SHE'S COUNTRY STRONG

A WILDER SISTERS NOVEL

HEATHERLY BELL

Dear Reader,

Have you ever made a very big, very public mistake?

Most of us have not. Many of our mistakes are private, thankfully, or at least between a handful of (hopefully forgiving) people. Certainly not hundreds of thousands of people. Honestly, I'm fascinated by those who must live in the public eye. It must feel as though your life is not entirely your own, and that's not fair to anyone.

Welcome to the second book in the Wilder Sisters series. This one focuses on the youngest sister, Sabrina, whose indiscretion meant the eventual demise of the Wilder Sisters band. Sabrina has a lot of making up to do, and she wants to start with her loving, close-knit family.

I love writing strong heroines, and say what you will about her, Sabrina Wilder is strong. Another word might be stubborn, or possibly headstrong, and I'll give you that. But you get the idea. She's been knocked down a time or two by life, and by her own mistakes, but you can't keep this woman down. She's made of strong stuff.

And then there's Damien "D.C." Caldwell, an alpha after my own heart. A rancher, a "fixer," and a man who knows what it's like to make a huge mistake. He believes his last job before he retires from his career as an image consultant will be his easiest yet. A tough guy himself, he's prepared to throw a Hail Mary pass over all the chaos and fix the problem itself.

But he's not prepared to lose his own heart in the process.

I hope you enjoy.

Warmly,

~ Heatherly

xo

1

"Hell on Wheels" by The Pistol Annies

Damien "D.C." Caldwell's first thoughts after arriving in Whistle Cove were that this was not a bad place to be banished to. If he had to run anywhere in the world with his tail between his legs, a good bet was that he'd pick a beach town if all things were equal. Probably in Mexico where it was warmer. For a California beach town, the Monterey Bay nestled along the central coast was damn cold for a Texan. It had to be in the fifties this late summer morning.

D.C. parked and unloaded his one suitcase out of the luxury sedan rental. The job here shouldn't take long. This was his very last assignment as a celebrity image fixer, and after this he'd be headed to the hot plains of Texas. Off the grid as far and as fast as he could get there. Frankly, he was sick of people. Entitled people. Talented people. Rich people. But he didn't discriminate. He was also sick of middle-class people. Young people. Old people. Hell, pretty much all people. He realized this didn't endear him to many, but ask him if he cared. He did his job, was good at it, and received a handsome payday every time he succeeded. He'd been saving and investing wisely for years and had a decent nest egg to retire to his own cattle ranch at the age of thirty-two. This might be his easiest assignment yet, considering the setting, and he looked forward to heading back to Texas and the ranch he'd made an offer on.

"Checking in," he said to the blonde young woman sitting behind the desk. A small country-western looking sign read: *The Wilder Sisters Welcome You to Whistle Cove.*

She stood and flashed him a toothy smile. "You must be Damien Caldwell. Welcome to Whistle Cove! I've got your room all ready."

She exuded more enthusiasm than he was ready for at this time of the day, or any time of the day, but he would let that go. He understood she was part of the now defunct Wilder Sisters band and recognized her from all the photos of the CMA-winning, chart-topping band. She was probably ecstatic he'd come to save her little sister's butt. Said sister had really made a mess out of her life and career, not to mention her sisters' careers, with her poor choices.

"Thanks."

He pulled out his wallet and handed over his license and credit card. If she was impressed by his Amex Black Card, she didn't show it. Good thing he was long past the time of his life when he'd tried to impress women with money.

"Sabrina is so excited to meet you. Oh, I'm Jessie by the way. Jessie Wilder. I was the drummer. Always in the back." She handed him a form to sign.

He nodded. "Call me D.C."

"Well, D.C., we've put you in our very best room, the Sea Captain, and I think you're going to love it. It's got a wonderful ocean view, a new Jacuzzi in the bathroom, and a hand-picked selection of our area's best wines. Wine and cheese hour is at four o'clock every day in the lounge." She pointed. "Our large breakfast buffet starts at seven, and you let me know if you need anything!"

"Great. Where's Sabrina?" he asked, signing the appropriate paperwork.

The sooner he got to work on repairing the girl-gone-wild image that had caused the lagging record sales, and thus the end of the Wilder Sisters act, the sooner he would get to Texas.

Jessie's smile slipped off her face. "Um, I'm not sure?"

He narrowed his eyes. "What do you mean, you're not sure?"

"I...I think she was expecting you this afternoon."

"I'm here now."

This was his tactic. He arrived earlier than anticipated so he could get a clear picture of exactly what he was dealing with and not just what his clients wanted him to know. Usually made his work go smoother.

"Um, okay, let me...let me just call her."

Huh. Clearly big sister was covering. Not a good sign.

Jessie picked up a phone and dialed then waited with a frozen smile on her face. And waited. "I'll...just leave her a message."

"That's not good enough. Give me her room number, and I'll go find her." If his voice was clipped and edgy, he couldn't help that. He was beginning to smell a rat though he didn't want to believe that this assignment was possibly going to take longer than he'd anticipated.

"She lives in one of the cottages around the B&B." She handed him the map of the B&B property and pointed to an area in the back, not far from the parking lot. She circled a cottage.

"She there now?"

"Where else would she be?" Jessie lifted a shoulder.

D.C. held up his wrist and glanced at his watch. It was nine o'clock, and he'd dealt with his share of musicians who couldn't rise before noon. But those days were over for little miss country. After dropping off his bags in his room upstairs, which was much nicer than he'd anticipated, D.C. headed to the cottage.

He knocked on her door. Once. Twice. Three times. Finally, the door opened, and a young woman with bed hair squinted at him. She wore a long tee that barely covered her thighs, thick socks, and nothing else. He realized this because her perky nipples were saluting him from behind the thin cotton of the worn tee. At any other time, this might have distracted him.

"Who are *you*?" she asked, pushing a lock of hair back.

Jesus. She looked sixteen, not twenty-six. "You always open the door to a stranger, kid?"

"You were knocking. A lot. And I have a headache, so I needed that to stop. Who are you, again?"

Shit. Was she hung over? He hadn't been notified of any substances abuse problems but family sometimes got it wrong. The drinking and the partying would be over with today, but if there was an addiction involved, this assignment would go from two weeks to six months. Not happening. He considered informing her he was her worst nightmare, but that would be too off-putting, and he needed her to cooperate.

But why wouldn't she want to revitalize her career and get back to Nashville? Her sister Lexi was already living there with her fiancé, Luke Wyatt, the latest country music sensation, and she wanted to get her little sister back in the business. He understood this was what Sabrina wanted, too. The jobs were always easier when his client cooperated.

"I'm Damien Caldwell. Luke Wyatt hired me. Get dressed and meet me in the breakfast area."

"Okay." She rubbed an eye. "When?"

"Now."

"Now? But I just got up. I need to shower, I need to...have coffee." Her voice got small and weak, leaving him to recognize all too well the pitiful sound of shame.

"Fine, do all that. Then meet me. I don't have any time to waste. We need to get to work." He hooked his thumb toward the B&B.

"Right." She quietly closed the door.

D.C. had a bad feeling about this. Every one of his nerves went on high alert. Sabrina's image needed an overhaul Luke had explained over the phone. She needed help dealing with the media in the wake of her sex scandal. The same one that had derailed the career of the Wilder Sisters band. Take a young girl and get her ready for a comeback since there was already interest in her brewing in Nashville. Easy job. Should have said no. Should have known better. Just his luck.

This wasn't going to be easy or simple.

Not this girl.

Not easy at all.

～

"BUT WE HAD a meeting set for this afternoon!" Sabrina complained to her sister Jessie on the other end of the phone.

She'd missed a call from Jessie just before the devil incarnate had arrived dressed like a billionaire in a business suit. Damien was the *perfect* name for him. Who was this dude? Where did he get off ordering her around and calling her a "kid"? He didn't look *that* much older than her.

"Next time, answer your phone when I try to call and warn you!" Jessie said. "You'll want to be nice to him. He's here to help you."

Their older sister, Lexi, wanted to help Sabrina get back to Nashville. This time, she'd be on her own since Lexi had joined Luke's band, and Jessie was not interested in anything but running the B&B. For a real shot at a comeback, she needed to repair her image for her fans. Big time. It had all been a huge misunderstanding anyway. Texting a photo of herself topless to a guy she'd thought she could trust had been an epic mistake. Huge. Not that she wasn't used to making them, but boy that one was a doozy. She thought she'd never live it down. Blowing up her career was one thing, but she'd torpedoed her sisters' careers, too.

Sabrina missed singing and dancing. Performing. Missed the true-blue fans who'd never turned on her. But now, she was a little scared. Right after the photo had surfaced, she'd been hurt that someone had played her. Hurt was quickly followed by dismay that she, who'd only slept with one man in her entire life, had been slut shamed by the media. Anger followed dismay.

And she'd been afraid since the first hate mail had started to come in. It had been her first look at how horrible some people could be to complete strangers. She didn't understand how her life, and a bad choice she'd made, had made people she didn't even know irate. She understood her sisters being angry, Gran and her mother, too. Instead, they'd rallied to her corner, being supportive even if she'd let everyone down.

Coming back to their hometown of Whistle Cove was

what they'd all needed. Together, she and her sisters had worked at the B&B that had originally been run by their grandmother Wilder. Now Gran was semi-retired, dating Sir Clint, a British Clint Eastwood lookalike, and playing golf in Carmel. Lexi was back in Nashville. Mom kept saying she would move up from Palm Springs, but that hadn't happened yet.

Sabrina was told she'd get a makeover of some kind. Image repair by an expert. Sabrina didn't like the idea of being repackaged and refurbished like some kind of product. Or a car. But she'd go through all the hoops because if that's what got her back to singing, that's all that mattered. She showered, dressed, and made a cup of coffee in the kitchen. Just enough to get her to the buffet where she'd load up on the stuff. Getting up before noon was for the seagulls. Or squirrels.

Her small cottage was similar to her sister Jessie's in that it was one of the former service personnel housing. She had a small living area with French doors that separated the one small bedroom, a kitchen in the rear of the house, and one bathroom. It was perfect for one person, and for now, it suited Sabrina's needs. The only issue was closet space. She had quite a wardrobe, accumulated over years of performing, even if she hadn't used any of those clothes in a while. Mostly this past year, she'd used disguises. For a while, the paparazzi had hounded her, trying to get a photo of naughty Sabrina "in seclusion." Thank goodness that was mostly behind her, and no one had bothered her in a while. Still, the costumes were actually fun at times. A little like performing.

A few minutes later, she entered the large breakfast area that had one floor-to-ceiling window facing the ocean. She saw Damien sitting alone at a table near the window, wearing a blue button up with the sleeves rolled up, revealing sinewy, strong forearms. She'd been surprised by how tall and imposing he was, like a football player and not a corporate drone. His Rolex watch caught a ray of sunlight just now spilling through the fog. Clearly, like her, he liked bling and could afford to have some. In-te-res-ting.

She sat in the chair across from him, and he gazed at her from under long dark eyelashes.

He took in her outfit and went from zero to sixty in seconds. "What the hell is that?"

"What do you mean?" She glanced at her outfit.

"Is this some kind of a joke?" His sensual upper lip curled to the side, and his rather impressive jawline tightened to granite.

"Don't you like it?"

She might have been pushing his buttons to wear her hippie costume, complete with blue tinged shades and white platform boots. But hey, he'd asked for it by barking at her before noon.

"Let me get one thing straight with you right now. I'm here to help, but if you don't want my help, tell me, and we'll both save ourselves a little time."

"Okay. I'm sorry, I—"

How to tell him that she'd started dressing in costumes when she was such a reviled person that she hated being recognized? And yes, it had been fun for a while. A little bright ray of light in the darkness that had been her life when everyone hated her. Plus, she didn't think she looked *that* awful in this. He ought to see her pilgrim lady costume.

"Do you want my help, kid?" Though framed as a question, he made it sound more like a demand.

"Absolutely." She nodded her head vigorously. "I sure do."

And don't call me kid. She'd save that for later. He didn't look receptive to suggestions from her at the moment.

"All right." He stirred his coffee and met her gaze.

His eyes and short wavy hair were dark, a chocolate brown that reminded her of brownies. She didn't know why because he didn't look sweet. At all.

"Were you drinking last night?" he asked.

"What? No!"

"Any drugs?"

"Of course not!"

Despite her denials, with no warning, he reached across the table, took her elbows in his big hands, and then examined her arms. He was...looking for needle tracks? Who did this man think he was dealing with? She was a Wilder, from the sweet and clean country music band that had won CMA awards and topped the charts. Make one little mistake and suddenly she was a heroin addict?

She pulled her arms back. "What are you *doing*?"

"Can't ever be too careful. You looked a little hungover this morning. And if you were an addict, I'd have to cancel this assignment."

She scowled. "Well, I hope you're happy now that you've manhandled me!"

Sabrina shifted a little in her seat, hating the sensation of being weighed and measured by this dude. It probably didn't much matter what he thought of her, since he simply had a job to do: shape her up into someone Nashville would want to work with again. It had something to do with image and learning how to deal with the press after her little "incident." Having been a country music girl since she was a *real* kid, she liked casual and flirty. Boots and flip-flops. Skirts and jeans. Beachy. She didn't know what he had in mind and hoped he wasn't going to mold her into a *Pretty Woman* clone. That just wasn't her.

"So what do I have to do?"

"You have to *listen* to me. Do everything I tell you to do with no arguments. We'll be fine then."

She sucked in a breath. "Wow. Okay. Whatever you say, *Damien*."

Talk about a power trip. Plan to take over the world much, Damien?

"Call me D.C. Everyone does."

"Humph." She preferred Damien, son of the devil. Fitting.

"I'll let you have tonight off. Tomorrow morning, we get started. Meet you bright and early, seven o'clock," he said.

"Seven? You mean in the morning?"

There was *the look* again, scary calm, like he might strangle her. "Yes."

She *hated* mornings. She would hate them even more with this guy riding her every step of the way.

But if this was what she had to do to get back to performing, she'd do everything the devil in a business suit said.

2

"Kerosene" by Miranda Lambert

The next morning when Sabrina's alarm went off at six, she honestly couldn't open her eyes. The night before, as usual, she'd been too wound up to sleep until about two. It was always a struggle to get to bed earlier than that. She'd been a night owl as long as she could remember, and for a while, staying up late was a part of her life on the road. Nowadays she stayed up late reading, watching recordings of their concerts and happier times, and listening to music.

She struggled to pull herself out of bed, knowing how important it would be to make a good impression. When he'd arrived, and she'd opened the door half-dressed and sleepy, she'd apparently resembled someone with real problems. So she would set him straight today. Dragging her feet out of her warm and cozy bed, she hit the shower, dried and straightened her hair, put on make-up, and had two cups of coffee. She almost felt normal when she locked her cottage door and walked the few steps to the B&B.

The sky was a gorgeous blue-gray, socked in by the fog that would probably not dissipate until noon. Seagulls and the occasional pelican squawked, and the comforting sound of the waves rolling in and out soothed her. Mornings were cold on Monterey Bay, even in the summer, but Sabrina liked it that way. So much better than the hot and humid summer days she'd experienced in Nashville and touring across the country. She'd been born and mostly raised here and on the tour bus since she was ten. But Whistle Cove was home, the only one she'd ever known.

The thought of leaving here again, this time on her own without her sisters to have her back, had a solid stone forming in her throat. She wanted to sing and perform again, but she wished it could be like the old days. The days when Daddy was still alive and managing the band. Booking tours. It was a good thing he'd been gone when The Scandal happened. Though she was a mama's girl through and through, she'd never liked disappointing her father. He used to joke about the last name Wilder, changed two generations ago from Wilsenski. But *his* daughters were the opposite of wild.

As she walked, she took in the joggers who were out this early on the beach. So the rumors were true. Good looking men jogged at the crack of dawn. The Wilder B&B had a private access beach, but it connected to the larger public beach that was empty now save for the joggers. She fixated on a particular jogger who grabbed her attention with his obviously steely butt and long muscular legs. Hoo boy. One of her biggest problems was that she liked men. Tall men, average men, short men, blonds, redheads and brunettes. She'd once crushed on a guy with green highlights in his hair.

Making her way inside, and not finding Damien, she walked to Jessie's office. "Morning."

Jessie jumped and turned from the filing cabinet, hand on chest. "Oh my god, don't startle me like that!"

"Ha! Didn't think I could do this, did you? I guess you're surprised I'm awake this early, huh?"

"Yeah, a little. Mornings are so quiet and peaceful around here. Nice."

"The devil asked me to meet him at seven a.m. sharp." It was currently one minute to seven. And she was on time. "Have you seen him?"

Jessie scrunched her eyebrows. "You mean D.C.?"

Sabrina waved a hand. "Whatever. Yeah, him."

"Let's go take a look."

Jessie wandered down the hallway that connected the lower floor of the B&B to the larger rooms that included their dining room where they only served one meal a day. But serve it they did, thanks to their wonderful, award-winning chef, Olga. Scones, muffins, cake, and one hot dish a day.

Sabrina sometimes filled in as a hostess, filling coffee cups and such, but never *this* early.

"Maybe he's having breakfast," Jessie said.

"I didn't see him." She yawned. "We ought to give Olga a medal for being up this early *and* cooking."

"She gets here at *four* every morning," Jessie pointed out.

"Why didn't I know that?"

Four o'clock was the time she'd be going to sleep many times on the road. Jessie and Lexi, too. And to think that some people got up this early all the time by choice. If it wasn't for Olga, who had been with Gran for decades, Sabrina would have to assume they were all wackadoodles. But Olga was perfectly sane and kind, one of Sabrina's admittedly few friends. Sabrina followed Jessie to the dining room where there were smatterings of their guests sitting quietly at tables. No Damien. Had he seriously forced her to get up this early as a joke? Because it was not funny.

But just as they were heading back to the office, Sabrina noticed the glass door that connected the B&B to their private beach open. In walked the man she'd seen jogging a few minutes ago. He of the incredible butt and long legs. Damien. He was all hot and sweaty and for the love of coffee...*hot and sweaty.*

Sabrina hadn't noticed her jaw gaping until Jessie shut it for her.

"Good morning, D.C.," Jessie called out. "Have a nice jog?"

"Yep. Good run."

"I thought you said meet at seven," Sabrina said with a clipped edge in her voice.

"Right. That's what I said." He started walking in the direction of the steps and the upstairs rooms. "Be back down after a shower."

"But...you said to be on time. I didn't make you wait."

"Exactly. You don't make me wait. I make you wait." With that, he was gone, taking the steps two at a time.

Sabrina thought for sure there had to be smoke coming out of her ears. Her chest puffed up in outrage. "Did you... did you *hear* that?"

"Okay, I know that was rude, but—" Jessie said.

"He's so *mean!*"

Wasn't he basically her employee? He was sent to do a job for her, but he acted as if *she* worked for *him.*

"I wouldn't say mean exactly," Jessie said. "I'd say...um, firm. Bossy. In control. Stern comes to mind."

It had always driven Sabrina nuts the way Jessie tried to

be the family mediator. She was the family peacemaker, always had been. Unfortunately, she often sounded like she was on everyone's side which was hugely annoying.

"Would you pick a side?" Sabrina went hands on hips.

"I'm always on your side!"

"It doesn't sound like it."

Jessie pulled Sabrina into a sideways hug. "Here, let's go call Lexi right now. It's two hours later in Nashville, and they've been in the recording studio most days. I'm sure they'll be up."

A few minutes later, she and Jessie were seated in front of her laptop on a Skype call.

"I miss you so much!" Lexi said. "Luke and I are leaving for the studio in a few minutes. I've got a new song. You want to hear it?"

"Yes!" Sabrina said. "Lay it on us."

Her older sister was always writing songs. Growing up, Sabrina had thought it was normal to have a sister who could come up with a song every day. Lexi had started off writing songs about her day at school, about the mean girl she didn't like, about the boy she crushed on. One day after school, Daddy came up with the idea that his daughters would form a band. Lexi would write the songs and play the guitar, Jessie would play the drums, and Sabrina would sing and dance. She was ten when this happened, and she'd been singing ever since then, traveling the world with her sisters. She'd learned a whole lot about performing and life on the road, but not much about boys or men. Once, when at home on a break from the road, she'd met Travis. He went to the same high school and had been her one and only on-and-off boyfriend until he'd been shipped off to Iraq.

Last she heard, he'd married a fellow soldier. Sabrina hadn't had the time for a boyfriend since Travis. Not that she'd had much time for him, either. That had been a part of the problem.

Now, Lexi played the guitar and sang a catchy tune about a sassy and wronged woman who was getting back at the man who had cheated on her...by slashing his tires and taking a bat to his windshield.

"This one's for you, Sabrina," Lexi said after she ended the song. "I still need a good title. Could be the first recording on your new album."

Jessie squealed and grabbed Sabrina. "It's just right for you!"

"Is the car a metaphor for something?" Sabrina asked.

"No, it's just a car," Lexi said.

"Why does she have to take a bat to it?" Sabrina worried a fingernail between her teeth.

"The bat is a metaphor for her anger," Lexi explained. "Well, do you like it, or should I go back and try again?"

"I don't know, it sounds kinda...mad?" Shouldn't she first come out with a song that sounded more apologetic? Sad? Sweet? Anger hadn't worked for her before. Had everyone forgotten?

"Aren't you mad?" Lexi said.

She had been mad before she'd gotten scared, and now she was simply ashamed. "I'm mad at Damien Caldwell."

She didn't want to sound ungrateful, but did he have to be so rude?

"Why?" Lexi said.

Sabrina started to explain, but in the middle of her explanation she glanced at the time. It was now 7:30, and she might actually be *late*. Oh, no, it would not go down this way. He would *not* be right. She was not going to get another scowl, quirked eyebrow, or scary calm.

"Gotta go!"

She ran out the office and down the hallway. Whew! She beat him. Yes, yes, yes! She wanted to jump and throw a fist in the air, but people were beginning to gather for Olga's breakfast buffet. She took a seat at a table closest to the entrance, smiling at guests, and positioned herself to watch Damien walk inside. Pulling on every one of her performing skills, she folded her hands in front of her and tried hard to look disgusted. Tight lips. Narrowed eyes. He was late. Yes, that's right, he was the late one. Uh-huh.

Unfortunately, when he stepped through the archway of the entrance, it was difficult to stay pissed. Also, difficult not to drool. She'd now seen him in a business suit and jogging shorts. Two very different looks, and he managed to pull off both of them. But now he wore a pair of jeans that were loose enough, but still accentuated his great behind, and a white button-down rolled up his incredible forearms. Those arms were man candy, and she might as well be a diabetic.

Look away, Sabrina. Look away. You hate him. You're off men.

She tipped her chin as he caught her gaze and seemed to give her the very briefest nod. Approval? She didn't know. Why should she even care? He made his way to the coffee, poured, and brought it back to the table.

"Much better look for you," he said without looking at her.

"Thank you." She thought he'd appreciate her summery pink halter dress with matching sandals. "I'm sorry we got off wrong yesterday."

I'm especially sorry you are such a jackass. Unfortunately, you're one of the best-looking jackasses I've ever laid my eyes on. This might make it easier to forgive your jackassery. The jury is still out.

"Same," he said in a deep and gravelly voice.

"So...how do we start over?"

He leaned back in his seat, hands splayed on his jean-clad thighs. "First, tell me what happened."

"You know what happened." So did everybody who had a radio, TV, or read a celebrity tabloid.

"I want to hear it in your own words."

"Really?" This might have come out sounding like a squeal.

"Really."

An almost unfamiliar sting of anger, not fear, coursed through her. But before he gave her his scary calm look again, she found the words to tell this man, this stranger, about the most humiliating time of her life.

"It happened at a party the label threw for us. There was this guy there, really nice and cute, and he wanted my number. I was getting ready to go on a tour, and I thought I'd like to see him again. It's hard to meet people, and I never really get to hang with anybody but our road and sound crews. Over the next few weeks, we texted back and forth, just friend type stuff. Then...then..."

"Go on."

She cringed. "Then it got a bit more sexual."

"Yeah?"

"He...he started texting me naughty things, but I kind of liked it. I like men, okay? Sue me."

He scowled. "No one's going to sue you, least of all me, so cut the attitude."

"What now? Do you want me to tell you what he *said*?"

"No." Scary calm again. "What I want is for you to tell me how you wound up sending him a photo of yourself half naked. That's what I want."

Oh, man. She felt a flush come on, her cheeks probably turning rosy pink, so she touched them briefly with the pads of her fingers, hoping to cool them down. "H-he asked for it. He wanted me to send him a little flesh."

"Do you always do everything men tell you to do?"

"No. But...I don't know a lot of men."

He studied her briefly, and then lowered his gaze to his coffee cup. "Fair enough."

"I thought I could trust him. Thought it was just for him—"

"But he sold it to the highest bidder." He nodded. "Kid, I know you've learned your lesson. Thing is, when someone is famous, there are always some who envy that fame. And beyond the envy, they hate that you have so much more than they do. They don't consider it fair. They don't think it's right. So at some point, if they have any advantage at all, they're going to use it. Either to hurt you, or to use you. Or both."

"We didn't even have that much money for someone to take," she tried to explain. "Not since my father died, and our royalties were cut because of streaming and stuff."

"Doesn't matter. You had fame, which is incalculable wealth to some."

She'd never really thought about it. For her, it had always been about the singing, the music, the high of performing with her sisters. Daddy had handled all the money, and he took care of his girls. Even now, Sabrina was just learning how to pay her own bills. It was embarrassing not being a real grown up-at twenty-six. Jessie was helping her with all that.

"Fame isn't important to you?" she asked.

"No." He shook his head. "Not to me."

"Then why are you doing this kind of work?"

"It suits me. Kind of fell into it at some point." He met

her eyes. "But you're my last job, so take it easy on me, yeah? Going to retire after you."

"You are? But you're so young."

"Thirty-two. Saved my money. Invested. No family, no wife."

No *family*? Sabrina nearly bit her tongue in half to keep from pursuing that line of questioning. Who had no family? She was suddenly very sad for him. Maybe this was why he tended to be a little abrupt. Stern. Don't forget rude.

"What will you do then, after you retire?"

"Got me some land in Texas. A cattle ranch."

He couldn't have shocked her more had he hit her with a cattle prod. She had no idea what that was, but it sounded painful.

"You're a *cowboy*?"

He did not look like a cowboy. More like a football player. Big. Manly. Huge callused hands.

"A rancher," he corrected.

"A rich cowboy, then." She settled back into her seat, enjoying this talk. Mostly because they'd stopped talking about her. "But do you have the boots?"

His lips twitched, and look at that, he almost...smiled? "I have a pair or two."

She did smile. "Of course you do."

He stood. "Ready?"

"For what?"

"Let's take a walk."

He turned to go, and she had no choice but to follow. She liked the view from back here much better anyway.

3

"Woman, Amen" by Dierks Bentley

S o far so good, D.C. thought. Sabrina didn't look much like a kid this morning, either, though she did appear a bit wired. He blamed that on the amount of coffee she'd probably been mainlining to be awake this early. But she'd passed his first test, getting up early only to wait. Hell, he'd waited for her, and he did not wait for anyone. Even if she had slid him a death look that should have buried him, were he a lesser man, it didn't bother him. She could throw all the hateful glares in his direction that she wanted, but if she didn't walk out, it meant she was serious. She cared.

Therefore he was in this. No addiction, no snotty nose entitled kid looking to skate out of any hard work. But she was more vulnerable than he'd imagined. Because he'd seen the video of the concert in Texas, during which she'd almost scolded the audience for daring to judge her, and he hadn't expected humble pie. Must have been her angry phase which was likely followed by fear. Fear that she'd lost everything she'd worked for. That was his sweet spot. He could work with that.

She liked men. News flash. Didn't need to tell him that. He'd noticed her checking him out, three times so far. Of course he'd done the same because he was human. She was beautiful, with long platinum blonde hair that fell almost to her waist and piercing green eyes. Perky breasts and long legs. She'd actually blushed, and he couldn't remember the last time he'd seen *anyone* blush. Pretty cute. He still wasn't interested because he never mixed business with pleasure.

But it wouldn't be the first time one of his clients had wanted to get closer. He likened it to what he'd heard about women falling for their therapists. There was a closeness and false intimacy from sharing the most humiliating time of your life with a stranger. He got that. And he'd never taken advantage of it. Sure wouldn't start now with this...kid.

"Where are we going, Damien?" She followed behind him, struggling to catch up to his longer strides.

"Call me D.C. And we're just walking on the beach."

"How's that going to help?"

He wanted the fresh air. This morning his run had been invigorating with the salty sea air and nothing other than the sound of waves crashing. It was hard to find this kind of peace. He'd only felt this way on the plains of Texas.

"It might not help you, but it will help me. Been to a lot of places but never to one this beautiful."

"Thanks. I was born and raised here."

He heard the hint of pride in her voice. "Thought you were raised on a tour bus."

"Well, pretty much, I guess. But this was always home base."

"Good choice." He clapped his hands. "All right. Fame lessons begin today."

"Fame lessons?" She laughed.

Just as he'd suspected, no one had ever trained her on dealing with the public. No wonder, since her parents had managed the band in the beginning, and she'd simply been put on a stage and expected to perform. No wonder she'd gotten herself into trouble. He fervently wished everyone pursuing or dealing with fame would be forced to take fame lessons. It worked with athletes. Why not everyone?

"Sound funny to you?"

"Yes, kinda. You have to go to school to learn how to be famous?" She stopped to kick at a huge piece of seaweed the ocean had deposited.

"No, but it's a good idea to learn how to deal with all the adulation once you're in the public eye."

"Okay, then. Lay it on me." She turned in a circle, arms outstretched, face turned up to the sky.

The girl was a natural performer. He'd met plenty of them, but with her there didn't seem to be an off switch.

"C'mon." He kept walking, and she followed closely behind. "We have a few things on the agenda. First off, I've scheduled a fitting for you this afternoon."

"Where?"

"Right here. Your cottage. The designer is meeting you."

"I have a designer?" She stopped in her tracks, hand to her chest.

"Yes, you have a designer."

"I'm sorry, but I can't afford that anymore."

Now *he* stopped in his tracks. "You can't aff—"

"I get a small salary, and I don't have to pay rent for now, but I still have a few bills. Things have been tough for us lately, though they're getting better. See, the B&B had been struggling with vacancies for a while. But Jessie and Gran say things are looking up." As she spoke she literally wrung her hands together.

He tried not to let that get to him and let her prattle on, a bit unnerved by her naiveté and genuine innocence. "Kid, this is all part of the package, and you're not paying for any of this. Luke Wyatt is."

She got wide-eyed. "Really?"

"Don't you have any idea of the kind of future everyone envisions for you?"

Someone at Rise Up Records had a real heart for Sabrina Wilder, and being with the same label, Luke had heard about the interest. They saw her as someone who could rise from the ashes more beautiful and well-made. It was his job to make her ready for the kind of fame he was almost certain she'd have. They weren't talking top of the country charts and Nashville. This was cross-over, Top 10 in the nation superstardom. That was where Sabrina Wilder was headed, if she didn't manage to screw it up.

"I just want to get back to Nashville and hang with my sister. Record a few songs."

"It's going to be a lot better than that."

"Wow. Why didn't anyone tell me?"

"Lesson number one. Listen carefully, not just for what people are telling you, but for what they're *not* telling you."

"Um..."

"Look. Luke isn't going to send someone like me out here, all expenses paid, unless he sees a huge future for you."

"You're that expensive?"

Interesting that she fixated on that and not on the rest of what he'd said. "Yes. Very."

"I guess so since you're buying the cattle ranch."

Why did she always divert to him? "We're talking about you, not me."

"Right."

"Second lesson. Don't trust anyone who isn't checked out first."

"Anyone?"

"You can trust me. I've been checked out."

"I know that. Luke said you really helped him and Lexi."

"Just one talk did it for them. Luke needs to control his temper. Lexi, too."

"So do I." She bit her lower lip.

"Yeah. The scene in Texas? That can never happen again. You don't get to scold your audience, no matter how tough things are."

"Third lesson. Social media is your enemy. Add me on every one of your social media accounts. I'm going to be watching you and what you do. What you share. What you post. Think of it as a doctor's check-up to make sure you're healthy. This is a social media check-up."

Her eyes narrowed. "You'll be spying on me, you mean."

"I prefer to think of it as monitoring but whatever."

"Yeah, whatever. It's *spying*. Even my parents didn't monitor my phone."

He quirked a brow. "Might have been a good idea." Hard to argue with that one.

"I can't let you treat me like a kid. I'm not a child. I'm twenty-six years old, and I don't like someone spying on me."

She looked ready to stomp her foot. He hoped he looked ready to spank her if she did because that's exactly how he felt. He had no time for her childish attitude.

"This is the deal. Want to back out now?"

She studied the tiny grains of white sand at her feet. "No."

"Sorry, but your life is not normal. Everything you say, and everything you do, is being weighed and measured."

"I can't be everybody's special snowflake, and I'm okay with that."

"Good. That's not the point. You're presenting an image on social media to those who do think of you as a special snowflake. Who you are but only some of who you are. Anything that's controversial keep out. Any causes you believe in, out. Politics? Double out. Get me?"

"I get it."

She didn't look happy about it, but then again who was? Social media was the scourge of their generation. Of society. He kept accounts because he was forced to do so and for no other reason.

He held out his hand. "Phone."

"You're kidding me." She gaped at him.

"No."

Through a heated and angry gaze, she stared him down, crossing her arms. "When do I get it back?"

"We'll see," he said, though he fully intended to give it back to her after he checked that there was no more sexting going on.

"This phone is my life." With jerky movements, she pulled it out of her pocket and forcefully put it in his hand. "I want it back."

"Tell you what. If this all works out, I'll show you a way to set up a private social media account for only a few close friends and family. Everyone will have to be pre-approved by me first."

She scoffed. "You sound like my keeper."

"As far as you're concerned, kid, I am."

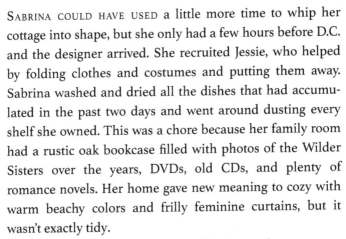

SABRINA COULD HAVE USED a little more time to whip her cottage into shape, but she only had a few hours before D.C. and the designer arrived. She recruited Jessie, who helped by folding clothes and costumes and putting them away. Sabrina washed and dried all the dishes that had accumulated in the past two days and went around dusting every shelf she owned. This was a chore because her family room had a rustic oak bookcase filled with photos of the Wilder Sisters over the years, DVDs, old CDs, and plenty of romance novels. Her home gave new meaning to cozy with warm beachy colors and frilly feminine curtains, but it wasn't exactly tidy.

"Did you know that this was all going to be so expensive?" she asked Jessie. "I had hoped to pay Luke back, but now I don't know if I'll be able to do it."

She was still trying to get over the fact that Damien was expensive. Now she felt even guiltier. First, she'd torpedoed the Wilder Sisters, and now Lexi's fiancé was paying for an image consultant. She was costing people money right and left. She didn't know how she'd ever fix all the damage she'd done.

"Not really, but I kind of assumed. I mean, don't worry about it, because Luke has the money now, and he'll do anything for us. Right?" Jessie picked up a pair of blue suede half boots with amazing four-inch heels. "Do you seriously need this many shoes?"

"Yes. I do." Sabrina wasn't going to argue the point. "Boy, I wish we didn't have to meet here."

Like all the former service cottages that dotted the main B&B, it gave new meaning to intimate. And she was going to be in this room with a designer she barely knew. After D.C.

had told her not to trust anyone not checked out. She assumed this designer had been checked out by Mr. Control Freak.

"How did it go this morning?" Jessie asked as she picked up another shoe and stuffed it into the dinky closet.

"He's so damn bossy."

"We already knew that."

But he made sense, too. She'd been on display nearly her whole life, but it had never been an issue until *men* were involved. If she didn't love them so much, she'd quit them. For good.

"He's going to monitor all my social media accounts like I'm a teenager or something."

"Oh." Jessie winced. "But it's not forever. Just for now."

"And he took my phone!"

"Oh, boy."

"I'm never going to send a topless photo again. Does no one believe me?"

"Sabrina, there are probably many other ways someone could take advantage of you. Maybe ways we don't even know about."

"Guess that's true." She picked up some of the folded clothes on the couch from laundry day. "He said never to trust anyone who isn't checked out. And that I should listen for what people are not saying, too."

"It's common sense, I suppose."

"How do I listen to what people are *not* saying?" She went palms up. "Be honest with me. Do you think it's a problem that I...find him attractive?"

Jessie squinted. "Anyone would find him attractive. You tell *me* if it's going to be a problem."

No one thought Sabrina was self-aware enough to realize her weakness for men, but they were wrong. She did.

And Damien was one hell of a man. He scared her a little bit, but another part of her was drawn to him with a sharp pull she didn't quite understand. She could write it off to his looks, but that wasn't everything. He was also arrogant, rude, and bossy. And yet... When he'd talked about being a cowboy, he'd seemed almost human.

"I kind of hate him, so that will help."

"Uh-oh."

"What does that mean? Uh-oh?"

"I think it's better if you don't *hate* him. You should be indifferent to him."

Indifferent? That would be like being indifferent to a locomotive train coming at her full speed. Stupid. "I don't know if I can do that."

Jessie sighed. "Do me a favor? Try."

By the time there was a knock on her door a couple of hours later, Sabrina was ready for the designer. She'd even made coffee and placed some of Olga's pastries on the small table by the couch. Maybe this could be somewhat relaxing because she did love clothes almost as much as shoes. And one of the things her daddy used to say about her was that she'd never met a stranger. She'd simply treat this designer like the friend she'd loved to have.

When she opened the door, there stood Damien next to another man, nearly dwarfing him. This man had spiky blonde hair with pink highlights, wore a red scarf, striped shirt, and skin-tight purple pants. Sabrina liked him immediately. She hadn't expected Damien, though she shouldn't have been surprised. Apparently, he also wanted input on her wardrobe. Next thing she knew, he'd be choosing her laundry detergent and her toothpaste brand.

"What are you doing here?" she asked Damien.

"Did I not mention I'd be coming along?" He moved past

her into the cottage, and the designer followed him, hauling in a rack of clothes on rollers. He hooked a finger toward the designer. "This is Eddie Black. He's the best."

"Hi, doll-face. Aren't you beautiful?" Eddie rolled the rack inside and then stopped, hand on hip. "Okay. Where do we do this?"

Damien didn't answer, and he appeared to be scanning the room for God knew what.

"In my bedroom?" Sabrina opened the French doors. "It's right in here."

"Great set-up. We'll just get you changed and with every outfit, we'll open the doors, so D.C. can have a look-see."

She glanced at Damien, who had just taken a seat, long legs spread out, one arm stretched out on the back of the couch getting comfortable like he intended to stay awhile.

"You mean you're going to approve my *clothes*?"

Behind her, she heard Eddie snort as he began unzipping garment bags.

"More like your costumes," he said.

"Again, you're going to approve my *costumes*?"

Scary calm again as he met her gaze. "Yes. That's right."

"I thought you said Eddie was the best." She wagged a finger at him. Did he or did he not trust Eddie's skills?

"He is, but between elegant and sexy we have a whole lot of wiggle room, so I'm here to make sure we land on the right side of sexy."

"Oh, I get it. You don't want me to look like a ho."

This time Eddie's snort sounded a lot more like a laugh.

"You're catching on, kid."

One of these days, he was going to stop calling her that. She couldn't take much more. Stepping inside her bedroom, she slammed the French doors. "That man!"

"He must really like you," Eddie said, holding up a beautiful and sparkly gold evening gown. "Anyone else talks to him like that, and he's long gone."

"I doubt he likes me. But maybe it's because I'm his last job. After me he's retiring."

"Girl, you must be a handful."

She giggled at that because Eddie was so sweet about it. Now *him* she liked. "That's beautiful." Sabrina couldn't take her eyes of the sparkle and sequins. If bling had a definition in dresses, this was the one.

He held it up. "This would do for award night at the CMAs or the Grammys. Got to prepare you for everything. Why not start with the bling, I say."

Why not indeed. She stripped down to her bra and panties, and Eddie helped her into the gown, which he then zipped up for her. The gorgeous matching gold rhinestone-studded shoes were strappy with three-inch heels, and she wanted to marry them and have their baby. The gown fit perfectly, a little tight around the behind (because she had one) but otherwise perfect.

"I love this!"

"So do I. Make room, Carrie Underwood, here comes Sabrina Wilder!" Eddie waved in a flourish. "Now let's go see what the big man thinks."

4

"Sober" ~ by Little Big Town

D.C. was nursing his irritation with Sabrina questioning yet again when he absentmindedly tugged on a piece of cloth that seemed to be stuck to the couch pillow and came face to face with a pair of black satin panty thongs. There was a fabric softener sheet stuck to them, like they'd just come out of the wash and hadn't been put away. He stared for a second, then dropped them back and stuffed them behind the pillow again. Unnerving. He did not like thinking of her as a woman. Her age didn't matter. She acted like a kid, and so he would treat her like one.

Kid, kid, kid. She's just a kid.

Don't you forget it, Einstein.

"May I present, Miss Sabrina Wilder!" Eddie said with his usual dramatics as he opened the double doors.

D.C. had told Eddie that he wanted plenty of coverage up top. Little skin showing other than maybe some leg. This dress accomplished that and a whole lot more. They needed elegant and classy, sexy but also sophisticated. A tall order. Even if the label was thinking of her as a sex symbol these days, Luke trusted him on this. He knew she would need her base to launch her into the star they wanted. And that base had seen little Sabrina Wilder grow from a child into a woman. That woman stood before him now, and she was stunning.

He nearly swallowed his tongue. "That's...going to work. Yes."

She turned in a circle, extending her arms, licked her lips and then flashed a wicked smile at him. His chest constricted. She didn't look like a kid to him anymore, and that really bothered him. He didn't know why.

"Yeah. Perfect. Eddie, you're a genius." He cleared his throat.

"That's why you love me!" He subtly shoved Sabrina back into the bedroom and shut the doors.

The next dress came out, too revealing for Sabrina's amazing breasts. A rack which people everywhere had seen enough of. Except for him, of course. He'd looked at the photo once. Once was all he needed. And he would still like to get his hands around the neck of the man who had sold the photo.

"Too much cleavage. Thought I told you the only skin I want to see is some leg."

He waved the dress away, a reject. D.C. was trying hard not to look, but the stupid French doors had flimsy white coverings that were practically see-through. Try as he might, his eyes kept wandering back to Sabrina's nearly naked body each time she changed. She had absolutely no effect on Eddie, which was why he was so great at his job, and D.C. hired him all the time. But she was having some kind of unforeseen effect on D.C. He palmed his face when he caught a view of her bending slightly at the waist to get out of a dress, revealing peachy fair skin and an amazing ass to match the rest of her body.

What the hell was wrong with him? She was burrowing under his skin, and he never allowed that to happen. He'd once worked with a former Miss Universe who had been in trouble, a gorgeous woman, and he'd not once felt this kind of pull. It was unfortunate for him that he and Miss Sunshine had some kind of amazing chemistry. She annoyed the hell out of him, as most people did, but along with that annoyance was a fascination and affection for her that he couldn't deny.

God, why me? Why now?

He was so close to retiring with a spotless resume for his years in this business. And for someone who'd had a scandal of his own in his past that he'd lived down, he didn't need an ounce of conflict as he rode off into the sunset on his horse. Alone. Because yes, that was his plan, to be alone. His horses and cattle, and some of the hired hands he'd need, would keep him company. He figured from time to time, he'd find a woman in town to take care of his needs. Other than that, he'd spend his life on the ranch, happy as a pig in garbage. Yep, that was the plan.

Stick to the plan.

Love didn't work. He'd seen it literally destroy his mother. Love made otherwise strong people weak. He refused to be weak.

Six more changes, six more hurried approvals so that he could get out of here and stop drooling, and they were done. Eddie left the approved wardrobe with Sabrina, and D.C. reminded him to send the bill.

"That's it?" Sabrina said at the door.

"This is a good beginning. On Friday, we have an appearance to make at a gala in Hollywood."

Her eyes got wide. "Hollywood?"

She really had no idea. He'd have to break it to her gently, same as he would Luke. Luke was footing his bill, so D.C. imagined the man would prefer a good result. He believed that she was pretty much done with Nashville, but that didn't mean she didn't still have a career left. A stellar one.

He left her and went to his own slice of heaven at the Wilder B&B. He'd missed their wine and cheese hour and walked back as couples were drifting outside onto the private beach. He had to admit that the soft sound of the waves was comforting, and once again, he understood the intrinsic appeal of the tiny hamlet of Whistle Cove. He managed to grab the last piece of cheese.

"Mr. Caldwell," a woman's voice spoke from behind him. He turned to see an elderly woman dressed elegantly in a dress with a shawl thrown around her shoulders. Her gray hair was in a Victorian knot on her head and her blue eyes were warm. "Welcome to the Wilder B&B."

He shook her hand. "I don't think I've had the pleasure."

"The pleasure is all mine. I'm Sabrina's grandmother. My husband's family and I used to run this B&B oh-so-many years ago."

"You must be Audrey Wilder."

He'd done his research. The grandmother had pretty much retired from running the B&B and left it in the care of her granddaughters. But when one by one they seemed to be leaving, starting with Lexi Wilder, he had to wonder who would be left to run this great place. He assumed Jessie would stay, since the word was she had no interest in returning to the music business.

"I hope you're enjoying your stay. We Wilders are a hospitable bunch. Especially our Sabrina."

"Yes, yes. That she is." He nearly bit his tongue in half. If being a sassy smart-ass was hospitable, she had the market cornered.

"My son, her father, used to say that Sabrina could sell ice to the Eskimos." She laughed softly behind her hand.

Wasn't that the damn truth. She was selling sex to him without even trying. "She is a bit of a handful."

"Don't let her get to you, now. She's a very sweet girl most of the time. Loves her sisters and is a mama's girl through and through. You'll meet Kit too, I'm sure. It's...inevitable."

She made it sound like death and taxes. Inescapable.

"I look forward to that." Not so much.

She sighed. "Yes, well...it is what it is."

Wonderful. "Mrs. Wilder, if you'll excuse me, I think I'm going to take a walk on the beach after I go upstairs and change."

"Good idea. It's a beautiful night, but make sure you wear a sweater. No one is prepared for beach weather on Monterey Bay. It's like autumn year-round."

Once upstairs he took a shower, ordered a pizza to be delivered to him on the beach, and slowly walked back. The seagulls and pelicans were gone for the day since there likely was nothing left to forage. This made the night even quieter, and save for the rhythmic sounds of the waves, he had the peace and quiet he craved. Now if he could just take his mind off Sabrina. She was a job, nothing more. Not someone special. He had a sudden epiphany and thought he had the answer to why this all seemed so different with her. She was his last job, and on some level, that had affected the situation. Just knowing this would be the last time, even if he'd grown tired, had to mean something. A sense of nostalgia. Yes, that was it. Thank God. He didn't have to worry. This all made perfect sense.

His perfect peace was interrupted by the sound of someone singing in the distance. The sound carried over the waves. As the sound drew closer, he recognized the song "Sober" by Little Big Town. And then he recognized the voice as belonging to none other than the woman he was itching to touch. Her voice was full and lusty, much different than her speaking one.

"Oh hey, Damien. What are you doing here?" She stopped on the dune right behind him.

"Looking for some peace. And quiet."

Super-sized hint. Take it and get out of here before I do something we will both regret.

"Ah, got it. But hey, I wanted to thank you for the clothes. I love them all. After you left I tried them all on again."

"Don't get them dirty. For special occasions only."

"Yes, *Daddy*."

Another internal face palm. Why, oh why, was he being punished this way?

"Which one should I wear to the gala? Is the gold one okay?"

"Yeah, that's fine." Maybe if he temporarily agreed with everything she said...worth a try.

"And don't get mad, but I went ahead and took that one you didn't like, too. I just told Eddie to send me the bill for that one."

"What? Why would you do that?"

"Why not? I liked it as much as the other ones. It's cute."

"It shows off your tits too much."

She pointed. "Ha. You said tits."

He glared at her. "Why are you doing this to me? Why do you have to challenge me on everything?"

"I'm not! Okay, look, I'll wear that one only in private. Like maybe with my man."

"Your man."

Who is he? Where is he?

"Someday. I'll have a man."

He exhaled in relief. "Sure you will. Someday."

"I will. Because I think I have a lot to offer a man. And I happen to like sex. Is *that* okay with you?"

His brain screamed that he'd had enough, and before he could stop himself, he grabbed her arm and pulled her to him. "Never say that to a man. Never."

She was now so close that he could see a gold specks in her green eyes. Those eyes were heated and challenging. Angry. They were locked in a staring contest with him. "Why not?" she finally said. "Does it make you nervous?"

He snorted. "Yeah, Sunshine. It makes me nervous. I'm shaking here."

"Bet you are. Know what I think? I think you *know* that I could rock your world." She said this softly and slowly, tipping up to move as close to his lips as she could.

As if she wanted him to catch every word and not miss one in the crashing sound of the waves. And he didn't, as each word hit him like a kick to the gut. He swallowed hard. Sliding his hand down her arm, he released her.

That was the problem. He'd finally identified it.

She's right. She would rock my world. I'd never be the same.

And he didn't want this. Any of it. Not when he'd finally solidified the plan he'd worked on for years. It had kept him clean and on the straight and narrow with a vision for the future spread out in front of him. He would have the second largest cattle ranch in Texas, second only to his sperm donor's ranch. After a while, he'd have the largest. Proof that he was more than the bastard son of a billionaire rancher.

"Yeah," she said. "You know I'm right."

He didn't speak. Simply glared.

"Um, pizza delivery?"

D.C. turned to see a kid with a pizza box in his hands and a smirk on his face.

"Yeah, right here." D.C. took out his wallet and handed the kid a generous tip. He accepted the pizza box.

"Yum. That smells good." Sabrina eyed him. "You know what else smells good? Victory."

With that she turned and practically ran away leaving him alone in the dark with the moonlight and his pizza.

5

"Good Girl" by Dustin Lynch

Sabrina ran back to her cottage, hoping that last victory statement didn't have him hot on her heels to argue who was right and who was wrong. Who'd won and who'd lost tonight. She hoped she'd done a good job of hiding her fear from Damien, because right now her heartbeat thundered in her ears like a rocket. He'd pulled her to him, but his grasp wasn't rough or hurtful. It was firm and enticing. He was so close and warm to the touch. Hard. Strong as an ox. His eyes were deep brown and shimmering under long eyelashes. Full sensual lips. And his *voice*. Low and deep like the sound of a bass guitar.

She didn't understand her feelings. This was different. The attraction and chemistry she had with him was not something she'd ever experienced before. She didn't know what to do about it because she couldn't blow this opportunity paid for on her behalf. All those beautiful dresses. A chance for a new contract with a label and a chance to sing again. She didn't know what the Hollywood deal was all about, but hey, if she had to get to Nashville through Los Angeles, she'd do that, too.

But she was a country singer first, born and bred. Down to her roots. Sure, she wasn't classic country, but she would never be anyone but a country and western singer. Her daddy had been a big fan of Willie Nelson, and she'd grown up around those songs. Reba McIntire. Dolly Parton. Lexi's songs were also country influenced, even if they had a strong pop slant, and Sabrina sang them with a little bit of kick and sass. But some people made fun of country. Country wasn't cool. She knew this because she lived in Whistle Cove and had grown up with some of those people.

"Somebody help me, my dawg just died," Billy Dixon, one of her classmates, would sing in a ridiculous twang.

She was *not* Hollywood. Those people would make fun of her, too, she was sure. The gala made her nervous as she wasn't used to being around the corporate types. In the past at those events, she'd always stayed glued to her sisters. She guessed Damien would help. He seemed smooth as a worry stone. Except tonight. She'd completely unnerved him with her words. Some of the tight control in his eyes had slipped, and she'd seen full-on desire and lust in his gaze. Of course, he'd probably rather be kicked in the family jewels before admitting it. But he'd stopped calling her kid, and she rather liked that. She wasn't sure Sunshine was that much better, seeing as he'd said it between gritted teeth, but for now she'd take it.

She took a shower and slipped into her favorite long tee. Right now he was just feet away from her on the beach eating a pizza. Alone. He didn't have to be alone, but damn if she'd risk going back now and not having the last word. She was stubborn like that. The pizza had smelled delicious. Tomato sauce. Cheese. Maybe some pepperoni in there. The smells were as enticing as he'd looked, standing alone, his back to her, staring at the ocean. Sometimes he acted like he'd never seen it before, like it was some strange and beautiful phenomenon. She'd taken it for granted for a long time, and it wasn't until she'd been on a tour bus for months that she'd grown to appreciate being home. Home to the crisp sounds of the sea. The seagulls and pelicans squawking. Hell, even the yucky seaweed that the waves carried back to the beach and she avoided stepping on. Whistle Cove, where the sea was cold and the sand on the beaches almost white. Monterey Bay attracted people from all over the world, but to Sabrina it had always been home.

Pulling a pillow over her head, she closed her eyes and tried to sleep, but all she did was toss and turn. She thought about Damien and her unnatural pull to him. Thought about those lips of his touching hers and of him losing some more of that tight control. If she ever got a chance, she'd wreck him in a good way. Ride him like a bronco. He'd probably appreciate that, seeing as he wanted to be a cowboy.

But for now, she'd do her best to stay away.

APPARENTLY, Damien hadn't been able to get a flight for them until Friday. So, for a couple of days Sabrina made sure to help Jessie and Gran around the B&B as much as she could. She'd always felt guilty that, while her sisters pulled their weight, Sabrina hadn't always known how to help. She still couldn't figure out how to get the fitted sheets on the beds. And sometimes when she'd dry and fold towels, a terribly boring job, something or someone would distract her, and she'd forget what she'd been doing. She'd wander around, looking for something important to do.

Like now. She was in the kitchen with Olga, but she had no idea what she'd come in here for. Then again, she'd been awake since nine, trying hard to get used to these earlier hours Damien seemed to adore.

"Have some coffee, sweetie." Olga canted her head to the French press that made the best coffee. "It's fresh."

"Oh, thank you." She poured some into a cup. Even if she hated the taste of coffee, it was ever so helpful to a night owl on a rooster's schedule.

"Sabrina, honey." Gran came up behind her, putting a hand on her shoulder. "You're leaving us today, I hear."

"What? Where? Why?" Olga asked.

"To Hollywood," Gran said proudly. "A big gala event with Rise Up Records."

"Oooh, *mija*! How exciting! Tell me if you see Denzel Washington."

Sabrina laughed. "I don't think I'll be seeing all of the famous people. It's not like they all hang out together in one big room."

"Ay, what a shame," Olga said. "I will miss you, sweetie."

"It's not like I'm leaving forever. I'll be back here the next day."

"And you will behave yourself," Gran said with a twinkle in her eye. "Around Mr. Caldwell."

"I don't know if I could behave myself," Olga said, fanning herself. "That man is so...I don't know...so..."

"Arrogant?" Sabrina supplied helpfully and batted her eyelashes.

Irresistible. That's the word you're looking for.

"Sabrina," Gran scolded. "He's our guest."

Sabrina sighed. "I know. Don't worry, I'll be good."

Gran lifted the lid of a pot filled with Olga's tasty oatmeal of raisins, cranberries and brown sugar. "A car is picking you two up to take you to the airport this afternoon. Are you packed?"

Ha! Was she packed? She'd been packed since two nights ago when again she couldn't sleep because of one Damien Caldwell. He was driving her crazy, interfering with her sleep patterns and dreams. This morning she'd woken with what she swore was the taste of him on her lips. He'd tasted like Scotch in her fantasy because he looked like a man who drank Scotch. Truthfully, she had no idea. He could prefer piña coladas for all she knew. But he could *kiss*. With plenty of tongue. Wow. In her fantasies, he'd been the best kisser ever. For all she knew he was a terrible kisser but probably not.

"Don't worry, I'm ready, and I won't make us late."

A few hours later on the ride to the airport in San Jose, and then while going through TSA, Damien barely looked at Sabrina and talked to her even less. She followed his lead like a good girl, which by the way, in case anyone cared to know, she was. One serious boyfriend in her entire life, people! One! Just because she liked sex, and talked about it, didn't mean she was getting any. Far from it. She settled into the middle seat of the plane, between Damien and a large businessman who had his laptop open until the last possible second. Damien took the aisle seat to stretch out his leg. Fortunately, it was a short ride to LAX, for which she was grateful, because there was nothing better than feeling like a packed sardine.

"Why aren't we flying first class?" she asked him. Seemed like he could use the extra room.

He didn't even remove his shades as he answered her. "On Luke's dime? We don't need first class. I'll use the money where it makes sense."

Oh. Well, it was rather nice that he cared so much about

her family. She appreciated that and had a short burst of tenderness bloom for him. It also helped that she was sitting so close to him she could smell his cologne. It was divine, and she was certain very expensive.

A few minutes before they took off, an actor Sabrina recognized from a Netflix long-running series was escorted onto the plane at the last minute. Turning, he headed out of first class toward D.C. and stooped in the aisle to shake his hand.

"My man." Bobby Lewis patted Damien's shoulder, then shook his hand. "Good to see you."

"Same," Damien said, still not removing his shades. Neither had Bobby.

Sabrina wanted some cool shades like that.

"Did you help him?" she whispered, leaning closer which meant she was nearly in his lap.

"Yep," he said.

She got the feeling down deep in her bones that she greatly annoyed him just by breathing the same air he did. Fine. She would stop talking to him. See how he liked that. When he got around to ordering her again, he was probably going to start up with the words. Until then, she'd give him as good as she got.

Dead silence, baby.

It didn't last long. At the airport waiting for their cab, she swore she saw Ryan Seacrest being dropped off. "Oh my god, oh my god! Is that...?"

"Probably," he answered, sounding bored.

Turned out, Hollywood was weird from this angle. The Wilder Sisters had played a few shows here in the past, but she'd never seen much of the place. They passed through downtown, and she saw crowds of people, some in costumes. Chewbacca from Star Wars, Princess Leia, Darth

Vader, and a man playing a guitar dressed in nothing but his tightie whities.

"Oh, look. The singing cowboy," she said, pointing. "I saw him once in New York City."

When D.C. didn't say anything, Sabrina slumped down in her seat. She felt like such a fangirl or tourist. But seriously, her world had been the inside of a tour bus, a hotel room, and the stage. That's about it. No time for anything else. Roll in, roll out. This was kind of a treat, although she doubted that Damien would allow much time to sightsee. All business, this one.

When they checked into the hotel, the desk clerk seemed to know Damien and flirted with him, which he didn't even notice. He still hadn't removed his shades, but he handed over cards and scribbled signatures like he didn't need to see anything. They had adjoining rooms on the fourteenth floor. The hotel was a big maze, and Sabrina knew she'd get lost if she didn't follow Damien everywhere. Even then, she probably still would. He walked so fast with long strides that she could barely keep up.

"Catch up, Sunshine," he said as he held the elevator doors open, the most he'd said to her in a couple of hours.

This time he hadn't said her new nickname through gritted teeth.

"I'm taking the second key card to your room," he said, dropping her off at her door and handing her a key card.

She tipped her chin. "Why? So you can barge in here when I'm half-naked and have your way with me?"

A single brow quirked above the rim of the shades he still hadn't removed. "Yes. Exactly."

He wasn't smiling though. She got the idea he was trying to be sarcastic. "I know what it is. You care so much about me that you want to barge in and make sure I'm not entertaining a man in that titty dress you didn't want me to have."

"Do me a favor? Never say titty dress again."

"You got it." She saluted. "I didn't even bring it with me."

He waited for her to open the door and then placed her overnight bag inside. Before he left, he removed his shades and propped them on his head. "I have to tell you something, and I'm not sure you're going to like it, so just listen."

She sure didn't like the sound of that. "What's wrong?"

"It's about why we're here tonight." He ran a hand through his hair. "There's some interest from the label for you to be a cross-over artist. They think you'd do much better in that market. Popular contemporary music leaning more toward rock. So the plan isn't to bring you back to Nashville to record. It's to set you up as a huge recording artist...here."

She backed up to the bed and plopped down. "But I'm country. Nashville."

"I get that, but with your looks and image, it would be much simpler if we just use the brand you have. Polish it up a bit. Make it work for everyone."

"The brand I have?" She stared at him. "What does that mean?"

He sighed and wouldn't look at her. "Bad girl."

"Bad girl? *Seriously*?"

The kick to her stomach wound its way to her feet. She was sick to death of one mistake ruling the rest of her life. And she didn't believe that Luke and Lexi would sign on for this.

"Constrained bad girl. A badass, like Pink."

She loved Pink as an artist, but Sabrina had never seen herself being like Pink. Their styles were so different. "Does Lexi know?"

"I doubt it." He sat next to her. "Luke hired me, and he trusts me to be the best at what I do, so he's pretty much in the dark about what the record label wants for you. But hey, this is huge. They have plans to make you into a megastar."

"But I...just want to go to Nashville with my sister."

"Look, you keep telling me you're not a kid anymore, and I believe you. You're a woman, and it's time to strike out on your own."

God, if she had a nickel. "I wish you would have told me this earlier."

"You haven't made this job easy on me. Figured telling you too soon would make this harder."

"So you lied to me."

"Didn't lie. Their interest runs deep. It wasn't until some of the things you said made me realize you wouldn't be happy with this. But give them an inch, and then you take a mile."

"Huh?"

"Tonight the negotiations begin, Sunshine. If they're impressed, they're going to want you. Once they want you, you can better call the shots. Got me?"

"Okay." She had to admit that made sense. They'd eventually understand she belonged on a country label. "I do this tonight, and then maybe I can negotiate what I want later."

"You're catching on." He studied her, catching her gaze, not releasing it. "Here's another lesson. Your fans will want to get close to you when you've got fame. They'll want to know about your personal life."

"Don't worry, there isn't one."

"There will be. Someday. Right?"

"Yeah." She hoped.

"Like I told Luke and Lexi, don't try to pretend you can

have a personal life like anyone else. You gave that up long ago. But you can control *what* they know. If your fans know a few personal things about you, they'll be happy and satisfied. They're less likely to press for more, for all the stuff you'd rather keep seriously private."

She nodded. "Like who I'm sleeping with."

"Exactly."

"Wait. Why are you telling me this now? Tonight is just industry executives, right?"

"Because I have a strange feeling after tonight, you might not be alone anymore."

"What? Really?"

"Tonight, everyone's going to see you for the knockout you are. You're beautiful, Sabrina. You don't know it, but you are."

"*You* think I'm beautiful?"

"Because I'm not a blind man."

She couldn't dismiss the sharp tingle of anticipation that pulsed through her. "You would see a lot better, too, if you took your shades off when you're inside. Just saying."

His lips tipped up, revealing an achingly gorgeous smile. "Fair enough."

"You should smile more."

"Tell you what. Do good tonight, and I promise you I'll smile more. Remember, keep your cool above all else. No matter what anyone says, mean-spirited or otherwise, let it slide right off your back. There will be people here tonight who might not want you to succeed for whatever reason. They might have another horse in the race, or maybe they're just jealous. Don't let them win."

Don't let them win.

And with those words, Sabrina Wilder prepared to take her life back.

6

"Get to You" by Michael Ray

Sabrina spent two hours getting ready for the party. She'd learned a lot about makeup through the years, first from Mama, and then her stylist when she'd had one. She could now do it all herself rather expertly. She applied a base, underlined her eyes for depth, applied a hint of mascara, and then false eyelashes before adding a hint of color to her mostly pale face. There wasn't a whole lot of sun in Whistle Cove except through a cloud cover. She guessed everyone here would be tan like Damien. As a last touch, she straightened her normally wavy hair until it was sleek and straight and pulled some to the side so her bangs almost covered her right eye. Another styling trick from the experts. Finally, she slipped into the beautiful sparkly dress that made her feel like a movie star. When Damien knocked on her door, she was ready for him.

And holy guacamole the man cleaned up well. Not that he had ever looked grubby, but at the moment he looked like a tall, dark, and sexy James Bond in his beautifully tailored black suit and blue tie. His brown hair looked like perfection, as usual, and she'd just bet *he* hadn't spent two hours getting ready.

"Wow. You look...amazing," she said, grabbing her clutch.

"So do you."

He held out his arm, and she took it, squeezing his bicep to see if it was as hard as it looked. Basically, she was copping a feel. She nearly made herself laugh out loud with that knowledge. For the record, it was as hard as it looked. Like steel.

"I'm nervous," she said as they walked the long hallway to the elevators. "It's been a long time since I went to one of these parties. And the last time I did—"

She'd wound up talking to a man who'd said he was a fan. He'd confessed a huge crush on Sabrina, and of course, she was flattered. She'd given him her number.

And the rest was her bad history.

"That won't happen tonight because I've got you."

He had her. A prickle of awareness shot through her as she wished that someday she'd have a man like him in her life. Someone who had her back all the time. She'd had that kind of protection and safety with her family. Her sisters. She knew she'd been luckier than most. The Wilders had been such a tight and close-knit family that they'd never had all that many friends other than work friends. Certainly, she hadn't. No one actually seemed to like her even though she was a friend to everybody, and she'd tried hard to be liked. Maybe too hard, at least according to her sisters.

Still holding on to Damien's arm, they entered the room reserved for the big recording label party. Awed by all the beautiful people, she couldn't help but feel inadequate in comparison. Most of the women were wearing stylish black evening gowns. Sleek. Sophisticated. Somehow her glittery gown felt like overkill in here. Like she was trying too hard again. She clung to Damien, who shook hands easily with everyone as he strode inside. He introduced her as Sabrina Wilder, neglecting to mention her prior association with the Wilder Sisters. This was good, she guessed, seeing as the sister act was a thing of the past. It still stung a little, since at one time, she'd imagined she and her sisters would be performing together all their lives.

She recognized some of these faces in the crowd. Many of them she'd seen at the Grammys accepting awards for their work. She was intimidated by this overachieving crowd. The Wilder Sisters had won a couple of CMA awards but never the coveted Grammy. That had always seemed out of their reach. And now, there was not one country and western singer who she recognized in the room. She supposed that was to be expected, but it would be nice to see some familiar faces.

"Sabrina Wilder," said a distinguished-looking man with salt-and-pepper hair and a nicely trimmed matching goatee. "All grown up. God almighty, girl, you look magnificent."

"Doesn't she?" Damien said. "Sabrina, this is Henry Thornwood, CEO of Rise Up."

Sabrina shook the man's hand. "I'm so happy to be here."

"Sabrina is getting back to work soon. She's been working on new material and should be ready to go into a recording studio soon," Damien said.

"For us, I hope?" He grinned, taking another flute of champagne from the passing tray.

"We're trying to arrange that, yes," Damien said smoothly.

He seemed like a different person tonight. Not the often

annoyed and arrogant man he'd been. And he was lying, too. She didn't have any new material, not yet anyway. She wondered if this was something he did often.

Listen for what people are telling you and also what they're not telling you.

Sabrina didn't know what to do with this information. Maybe Damien was simply selling her, presenting her, and he probably was using everything in his arsenal. He was the expert here, not her. She still didn't like it.

"How do you feel about popular rock music?" Mr. Thornwood said. "Who are some of your favorites?"

She squeezed Damien's forearm, but not to cop a feel this time. It was to release the pressure and tension she felt trying to come up with someone's name. Her idols had all played at the Grand Ole Opry. But she had definitely listened to cross-over artists.

"Luke Wyatt," she said, because Luke had recently had such cross-over success with the song he and Lexi had co-written. "And I love Sam Hunt."

C'mon, who didn't?

"That boy sure is moving country in a whole other direction, isn't he? Sure wish we'd signed him." He sighed and chugged the rest of his drink.

"She likes Pink," Damien added helpfully, saving her butt.

"Good choice. I think she's here tonight. Somewhere." Mr. Thornwood scanned the crowd. "If I see her, I'll drag her over for introductions. She's a real sweetheart."

"That would be awesome."

Pink! She'd forgotten how much she liked the power singer and her kickass songs. If she got to meet her, she hoped Damien would be nearby to keep her from fangirling too much.

They made the rounds, and Sabrina met so many industry insiders that the names blurred. Faces she could do, but names were another story. Damien seemed to know everyone's name and made it a point to make them realize he remembered them. And they looked impressed. Especially the women. Sabrina didn't miss the way some of them took him in, like he was a slice of cake that wasn't on their diet. Too many of the women looked like they could use a sandwich. Sabrina had never thought of herself as fat until tonight. Curvy, yes. These women didn't have waists, and they also didn't have butts. They were one long strand of beauty.

"Be right back," Damien said and parked her near the champagne display.

"Nooo," she whined, holding on to him for dear life.

"Sunshine," he said with his scary calm, "I said I'd be right back. I need to talk to someone."

"Fine." She let go of him, and he crossed the room with purposeful strides.

It was time to perform. She'd done plenty of that in her life, even on days when she had the flu and wanted to crawl back into bed. From the time she was ten, she'd been taught how to be a professional. To smile even if you didn't want to. Sing even if you just got dumped by your boyfriend because he was headed to Iraq. Dance because everyone was always watching. Sabrina picked up a flute and used it as movie stars used cigarettes for the cool factor a long time ago.

She pretended she was Grace Kelly, one of Gran's favorite movie stars. Putting on a smile, she slid it to everyone who looked in her direction. Tossed her hair. She caught the eye of a few men, not her intention, but finally a trio of women moved toward her as if they would say hello. Sabrina said hello first and got ready to make a friend or two, but they kept walking past her, stopping only a few feet behind her.

"If she thinks she can come to Hollywood just because she's scandal-worthy, she'd better think again. They're only signing two new artists this year."

"Maybe I should sell a topless photo of myself to get notoriety, too. You have to admit, it's a cheap shot but some genius marketing."

"All I know is you can slap lipstick on a pig. It's still a pig," another said.

If Lexi had heard these women, she'd have knocked them out with one swift punch. If Gran had heard them, she'd have washed their mouths out with Ivory soap. If Jessie had heard them, she'd probably have tried to convince they were wrong by talking their ears off. But it was Sabrina who'd heard them, and another slice of her heart broke off. They knew Sabrina could hear them. This was all for her benefit. Obviously. The old Sabrina would have launched into a tirade of her own, but that part of her had been quieted and shamed a while ago. Still, she was strong enough to want to defend herself, even here. She turned to face the cowards and gave them a look that could kill. They simply smirked and sneered.

There will be some people who won't want you to succeed.

They might have another horse in the race.

Or they're just jealous.

But Sabrina didn't believe these beautiful women were jealous of her. Their eyes said it all. She didn't belong in this Hollywood scene. All along, she'd known she wouldn't. But now it hurt, harder than she'd expected, and the pain slid into her like a sharp memory. Because she still wanted people to like her, still ached from a time when the whole world hated her. This wasn't much better. Did they honestly

believe she had done this on purpose for all the bad attention? All the negative publicity? They didn't judge her for
her indiscretion, but because they thought she'd used The
Scandal to get ahead. They didn't *know* her or her family.
Didn't know that she'd let them all down which had hurt
her the most. In her life there had always been just two
things: family number one, and music number two.

Horrified, she felt her eyes sting. A sob threatened to
push through her tight chest. The walls seemed to be
closing in on her as she stood in this huge room alone.
Unable to breathe. She couldn't stand here another minute
and pretend that she was like these women, or that she
would ever want to be. Setting her flute on the table,
Sabrina ran out of the room.

D.C. HAS JUST FINISHED TALKING to a few people he wanted
to introduce Sabrina to, but first he'd smoothed the road for
her. Talked about all the interest surrounding her, the revi-
talizing of her career. The comeback. Yes, he was going a lot
further and beyond what he would normally do for a client.
The way things were going, the executives acknowledging
their interest to him, he thought after tonight Sabrina might
eventually have a bidding war to get her signed. But when
he turned to check on Sabrina out of the corner of his eye,
he saw her leaving the room. Not leaving.

Running.

"Excuse me," he said to the two men and one woman
who headed up publicity for Rise Up.

Fury dripping off him, he followed Sabrina out of the
room. She was nowhere in sight. This was completely unac-
ceptable. Had he not told her to let any insults slide off her

back? He hadn't heard any, but when he'd passed a small coven on his way out, he had his suspicions. Jealousy, pure and unbridled. Not one of them had the charm of a Sabrina Wilder. She presented as a fresh ingénue because she was. No one else in this room could pull that off.

Now she'd ruined his plans for her tonight by again not listening to him. Challenging him as she did at every turn. Maybe now he'd simply be done. Wash his hands of this mess. Just explain to Luke that he couldn't work with someone who wouldn't take his advice. And he'd tried. God knew he had. He punched the up button on the elevator with more than a little anger. With every floor he grew more livid.

Calm down.

Why did it matter so much? If she wanted to torpedo her career, it wasn't any of his business. But he knew why. She got to him. Try as he might, he couldn't get past the fact that she saw *him*. She saw past the stern attitude he gave her and treated him as if he was someone else entirely. Because of that he'd grown to give a shit, something he'd promised himself never to do again. The blow of that knowledge hit him square in the chest. He deserved whatever he got for getting invested. The toughest lesson of all had once taught him not to get invested at all. Even in those who supposedly loved him unconditionally.

He knocked on her door, and when she didn't answer, he pulled out the extra key card and let himself in.

"Sabrina!" he bellowed, sure he sounded like a crazy man.

To hell with cool and collected. At last he'd get through to her. She wasn't in the room, but he heard the water running in the bathroom which not only terrified him, but made his boiling blood grow suddenly ice cold. He knocked on the bathroom door once. Twice. Then turned the knob. He'd never had a client lose such faith in their future to the point of hurting themselves, and the thought of Sabrina being the first made his panic grow exponentially until he would have torn the door off its hinges if it had been locked.

Not giving a hot damn about anything else right now, he flung the shower curtain back to find Sabrina Wilder, his favorite spitfire and hell on wheels, sitting on the floor of the tub fully clothed. Deep guttural sobs shook her frame, but she was whole. She wasn't hurt or injured or bleeding.

D.C. allowed himself to breathe again. "Sunshine."

She acknowledged his presence by ducking her head under an arm and turning to the wall. The gut-twisting sobs didn't stop. They continued on, and to him they felt like short jabbing stabs to his chest. He wanted more than anything for her to stop. He'd do whatever she wanted if she would smile again and sass him and tell him she wanted the titty dress.

Hell, he'd let her wear the freaking titty dress to break- fast if she'd stop making his chest feel tight. He didn't wait for her to face him. He didn't wait for her to stop crying. He waited for nothing and no one as he reached to shut off the faucet, tugged her out of the shower, removed the dress and her underwear, threw a towel on her and carried her out of the bathroom. Then he simply sat down on the double bed and held her on his lap.

Not knowing how else to comfort her, he simply rubbed up and down her naked back. She positioned her arms around his shoulders and buried her face in his neck. He didn't try and get her to talk to him. There would be no point. He wouldn't understand a word she said anyway. At the moment, every bit of oxygen she had was being used, taken up in the matter of crying like someone had ripped her heart out. He didn't know how long he'd held her, gently patting, rubbing her legs, anything to offer comfort, when the sobs began to subside.

So there was a God. If he'd ever had doubts before, this ended them.

"I'm s-sorry," she said when she could formulate a word.

"Don't talk, baby."

He would have preferred not to find out that Sabrina was still hurting from the hell she'd been through. His first mistake had been to believe she was stronger than this. He'd believed it because of her carefree attitude but it was clear she wasn't over the past at all. It had been nothing but an act. It was also clear that he'd lost control at some point and let her in. He wondered when exactly that had been. Wondered if it had been the first day he met her, when he'd stayed despite his doubts this would be easy, or when she'd brazenly told him she liked sex, and that she could rock his world.

Or maybe it had been when he heard the sound of her lusty voice singing, mixing with the sound of the crashing waves, and filling the silence he'd thought he wanted.

7

"Speechless" by Dan & Shay

When Sabrina had calmed down enough to simply hiccup instead of sob, D.C. stood, threw back the covers on her bed, helped her lose the towel, and covered her gently. She stared at him with a mixture of fear and awe. Oh yeah, he still had his slightly damp suit on. Tie. Everything. He removed the jacket, loosened the tie. Then he made his way to the phone.

"Yeah, we need some dinner here." He picked up the menu and eyed it. Then he ordered nearly everything on it. Sue him, he was hungry and traumatized. "And a bottle of Scotch."

"Y-you drink Scotch," Sabrina said from the bed, where she appeared half buried.

All he could see was her little face.

"Sure do. I ordered a bottle, didn't I? What'll you have? Yeah, that's a joke. I'm kidding." He shoved a hand through his hair.

"I'd like a hamburger, please."

"Would you settle for filet mignon?" He tugged the tie off and set it on the nightstand. Pulled the tucked in white button-down out of his slacks and rolled up the sleeves. "It's one of the many things I ordered off the menu."

"Sure."

He sat on the side of the second bed, facing her.

"You never joked with me before." She made this sound as unbelievable as hearing that little green men had been located on Mars.

He scrubbed his chin. "Guess I only joke when I'm nervous."

"Oh, me too."

He'd decided not to ask what had happened tonight minutes after finding her in the shower. It was enough to know that she wasn't ready for Hollywood, and he didn't know if they were ready for her. He'd work on Plan B. Sure, normally he'd exit stage left at this point. After all, he had a cattle ranch to get to. A lot of quiet and isolation waiting for him. He refused to ask himself why he wasn't leaving.

"Plan B," he said, spreading hands on his thighs.

"I'm sorry that I ruined tonight."

"Having second thoughts about tonight myself."

She went up on her elbows and brought the sheet up with her to cover her breasts. "I thought you said negotiations begin tonight."

"True. Negotiations have been relocated, that's all. I plan on starting a bidding war for you."

And while he realized he'd seamlessly moved from image fixer to publicist to manager/super-agent, he didn't much care at this point. He was knee deep in this.

"A war? That doesn't sound good."

"It's the best possible scenario. You ought to be able to choose where you go. Write your own ticket."

"Nashville?" she asked, her eyes shimmering.

"Anything you want, Sunshine."

A few minutes later, he was reclined on the bed next to hers, planning her comeback in his head when room service arrived.

"Damien," she said softly. "I'm naked here."

"Hide," he said with a chuckle. "I'm kidding. I won't let them all the way inside the room."

Carts arrived filled with trays and enough food to last them two days. He tipped the poor man generously, rolled the carts in, and closed the door. Sabrina was a lump on the bed.

"He's gone," he announced.

Her little face peeked out again. "Still naked here."

"Oh, yeah. Right."

She didn't want to eat naked. Might spill something on that peach-colored, flawless skin. A crime. "*Now* you're shy with me. Okay. Won't look again. I'm turning my back, go and grab something from your bag."

He was good about not peeking even if he was tempted. One of his favorite parts of a woman was her smooth and soft skin. And Sabrina had plenty of flesh, especially on that perfect ass, which looked far better without clothes hindering it.

Oh yeah, he'd noticed.

"Okay. You can turn around," she said after a couple of minutes.

He turned to see her in the same big tee shirt that came down to just below her thighs. The one that she'd worn on the morning they'd met.

"I thought I'd be sleeping alone, so I didn't bring anything else to wear for bedtime." She made her way to the carts and lifted the cover off of a plate.

"You are sleeping alone," he said, more for his own benefit than for hers. He would not cross the line.

Another line, he meant, because he'd already crossed a few.

~

SABRINA COULDN'T FIGURE Damien out. He drank Scotch, as she'd suspected, and though she still didn't know if he was a good kisser, she did know a couple of other things. Even if she thought he'd be furious with her, instead he'd been kind. Tender. And now, he appeared to be on her side one hundred percent, without regard for what he knew the Rise Up Hollywood division wanted from her. To have someone besides her sisters finally have her back felt incredible.

She watched him now as he drank his Scotch and ate his steak. He was hungry, he'd finally admitted, and frankly, she was starving. A good cry always made her first exhausted and then hungry. She hadn't cried like that since The Scandal, like she'd been saving it all up and couldn't keep it inside anymore. In the beginning, she hadn't cried because her immediate reaction to the photo had been defensive.

She hadn't wanted to believe *she'd* done anything wrong. It had been the man who betrayed her who'd been wrong. But then, she'd finally had to admit to herself she'd been at least partly to blame. She'd given the man ammunition, trusting someone she hadn't known well enough. Dying for some affection and attention from a man because she'd been so lonely on the road.

So damned stupid.

Tonight she'd cried for everything. For the betrayal by a man, for ruining not only her career but that of her sisters, for feeling so lonely all the time, and finally because she had a mother who stayed away too much. Sabrina under-stood she'd stayed away because she didn't much like the new reality. A world without her husband. One without music at its center and a B&B instead.

Her mother didn't quite understand how much Sabrina had needed her in those early days after The Scandal. It didn't matter as much because she'd had her sisters and Gran. But recently, even that had been taken away when Lexi went back to Nashville with Luke. It was only fair. They were getting married. She'd known this would happen and that they'd all move on. Her sisters would have their own families. And so would she. Someday.

"You okay?" Damien asked, as if he wanted a check on her emotional state.

She took a bite of the creamy mashed potatoes and cut into her filet mignon. "I'm good."

He met her gaze. "Not going to lie. You scared the piss out of me tonight."

"I thought you'd be mad."

"Oh, I was mad. And then I was terrified."

"You're *that* afraid of a woman crying?"

"No," he said, downing some Scotch. "I thought maybe... maybe you would hurt yourself."

Now she felt horrible. Poor Damien. "No, I would never do that."

"How would I know?"

"I'm sorry. You don't know me well enough. That would never happen."

"At some point, everyone reaches their desperate side. What I know about you is that you're difficult and feisty. Sexy and damned talented, too."

"Wait. Sexy?"

He ignored that. "I just thought you were stronger."

She sat up straighter. "I *am* strong."

"Told you not to let them win."

"And they didn't." She tipped her chin. "I had a real good cry that had been a long time coming. I once read that kind of a thing can fester inside you and rot you from the inside out, so I should probably thank them. I'm sorry about the dress, and your suit, scaring you, and everything. But I'm the one having a room service dinner feast with a devastatingly sexy man, so who's winning now?"

He quirked a brow.

"You think I'm sexy, and I think you're sex on a stick, so what are we doing to do about that?" she asked.

"Nothing, if I can help it."

"Why? Why do you want to help it?"

"It's unprofessional. In all my years doing this work, I've never slept with a client. And it's unethical. Most of my clients are going through a rough patch. Emotionally, they can be in shambles. Definitely in a bad place. That's when I come in and start repairing. It would be unfair to take what I want."

What I want. She sat with those words for a long luxurious minute. "It's different with me." Surely, he could also feel the chemistry between them, the sexual tension as thick as her steak.

He didn't deny it.

"How did you get into this business, anyway?" she asked.

"Had my own scandal."

This shocked her to the core. He didn't look like the type of man who would ever make a mistake. More like one whose every move was planned and scheduled ahead of time. It was good to see a facet of his human side. He'd once made a mistake. Probably a big one.

"What kind?"

"Short story? I was on a football scholarship to Texas A&M. Full ride. One night I drank too much and got pulled over for a DUI. Arrested. Lost my scholarship."

"I'm so sorry."

"I'm lucky no one was hurt. Anyway, I completely reinvented myself with the help of my mentor. Went back to school and got my degree. After that, I wanted to do what he did. Help people who'd made a terrible mistake with the second chance almost everybody deserves. Almost."

"Not everyone?"

"Some of the people I've met and worked with? Not sure they did. Eventually, I turned some assignments down because I didn't need to take them. I could pick and choose who I worked with, and I somehow lucked into working with celebrities and folks in the music industry. Not saying that every one of them deserved a second chance, either. I grew to hate people. I think it's because I've seen too much of the worst side of people. The part I help them hide from the world as they reinvent themselves and learn how to deal with the media of today."

"What part are you helping me hide?" She was curious as to what he saw as her worst side though she definitely had some idea.

He met her eyes straight on, unblinking. "That would be what you told me on the beach. You like sex. You don't care who knows it."

"I should care who knows it," she said slowly, even though she didn't just talk to *anyone* the way she had to Damien.

It was just too easy to rile him. Too easy to tease him, and yeah, she'd had her fun.

"You're too trusting. Too open with people. Be more guarded." He swallowed some more Scotch then slid her an irritated look. "And why the hell aren't you intimidated by me? Everyone else is."

She got the feeling that really bothered him. Worse, she didn't have an answer except the fact that she'd been through worse than Damien Caldwell. Plus, he was easy on the eyes, a special weakness of hers. But it was far more than that. She'd never had anyone truly see who she was before this and call her on it, too.

"Who says I'm not?"

He scowled at her.

"Okay. You see? I *am* strong not to be intimidated by you." She put some steel in her spine.

He stood up and stretched. "Our plane leaves tomorrow. We both need to get some sleep. And I have some calls to make."

"Stay with me a little longer," she said. "Please."

"What for?"

"Um, I want to watch a movie."

He picked up the remote and started going through the process. "Fine. This is how you do it."

"No, I mean I don't want to watch it alone."

"Why? Is it a scary one?"

Now she quirked an eyebrow. "What's with the fifth degree?"

He held out his palms, giving up. "Let's watch a movie."

She picked the romantic comedy over the action thriller he preferred, and he only groaned a little bit. After all, watching a movie had been her idea. Only thirty minutes into the film, Damien closed his eyes and his breathing became regular and even. He'd fallen asleep in his clothes on the bed next to hers. She studied his relaxed face, the strong jawline, and full lips. It would probably be best to

wake him and send him to his room where he could change
and get a better night's rest.

On the other hand, he seemed so peaceful already.
When the movie ended with the happily ever after she
needed tonight, Sabrina shut off the TV, covered the food,
and turned off all the lights. Then she quietly, as stealthy as
a cat, climbed onto Damien's bed. She didn't get close
enough to touch him. Just admired him sleeping, wondering
about his life, until she couldn't keep her eyes open any
longer.

WHEN RAYS of dawn sunlight spilled through the blinds,
Sabrina forced one eye open. She was still on the bed with
Damien, but now his arms were around her and her back
was pulled to his front. *Oh boy*. She didn't want to move at
all, maybe ever again, but pretty soon she'd have to use the
facilities.

Uncomfortable though she was with that need, she
didn't move a muscle until she felt Damien shift his weight
against her a few minutes later. He rolled to his back and
groaned. Then cursed under his breath. She only dared
open both eyes when she heard him rise from the bed. And,
oh my goodness, he looked so endearing in the morning.

Hair adorably disheveled, sexy stubble going into overtime now, sleepy bedroom eyes. Totally sigh-worthy. She
may have sighed.

He caught her staring at him. "I fell asleep."

"I know. And I didn't want to bother you."

He scratched the stubble on his chin. "You didn't want to
bother me, so you laid your half- naked body next to mine
instead of sleeping in your own bed?"

"Ah, you caught that."

"You're lucky I didn't do something about it."

"Uh, no, I am *not* lucky." She stretched. "Would you believe me if I said I needed the warmth of another human body to help me sleep?"

He fiddled with the coffee machine. "I'd say you're reaching."

"I don't know why you won't just let this happen." She tore the covers off and flounced over to join him. "I want you, and you want me."

He studied her from underneath his eyelashes. "I already explained why."

"I won't think any less of you. And I won't tell anyone. I pinky promise."

She only wanted him to kiss her. Just once to see if it would be as explosive as she thought it was going to be between them. Then she'd leave him alone. Sure she would. He actually gave her one of his better smiles, the one with his eyes involved, and leaned forward to tuck a hair behind her ear.

"While it's hard to turn down a *pinky* promise, I think we both better get showered and dressed."

She'd put him through enough last night, and they sure didn't want to miss their plane. Sabrina did as he ordered even if she didn't like it very much.

8

"All on Me" by Devin Dawson

Sabrina realized they had to be at the airport two hours before their flight, but she didn't understand why Damien pushed to leave the hotel so early. She had her answer when he showed up after she'd showered, dressed, and packed her bag.

"Leave your bag there and come with me." He held out his hand.

She took it of course. "O-kay. Where are we going?"

"We don't need to check out until noon anyway."

"So, why were you hurrying me?"

"I've booked us a tour," he said as they rode down the elevator. "Think I didn't notice the fan in you? You were practically hanging out the window to catch Seacrest's eye."

"Fine, go ahead and make fun of me. I've never had a chance to actually see the town itself. Just perform."

"Thought so. A common story."

Damien had booked them a two-hour tour on an open-air

bus that started at the Hollywood Walk of Fame. They walked on the sidewalk, stepping on the brass stars embedded with hundreds of famous names. He took pictures of her hamming it up. The bus was small, and he took her hand as they found a seat. On board with them were mostly couples, many of them obviously tourists speaking in other languages.

"This tour hits all the major tourist spots, and we'll wind up back here again at the end," Damien said. "Then we can go get our luggage and head to the airport."

Delight bubbled inside her as she realized he'd done this for her. She didn't think anyone had been so sweet and thoughtful in years. "Thank you."

He cleared his throat and looked away. "Didn't want you bitching at me later."

She squeezed the hand that she was still holding. Because apparently hand holding didn't cross his ethical lines. And she was okay with that. The tour took them through Rodeo Drive, the Sunset Strip, Grauman's Chinese Theater, and the famous Hollywood sign on the hill for photo-ops. Damien took a few selfies of them with the sign behind them, making her feel like part of a real couple. She grinned into the camera like a hyena while he looked serious as usual.

They were driven past a few celebrity homes and finally deposited back on the Hollywood Walk of Fame. Sabrina wandered into a gift shop and picked up two fake small Oscar trophies. By the time she was done shopping for Olga and everyone else, they had to run back to the hotel room to check out and get to the airport on time. They barely made it.

Sabrina didn't think she'd ever had a better day. Even though this technically wasn't a date, she reminded herself.

They were sitting on the plane, holding hands again, when a young passenger came up to them.

"Aren't you Sabrina Wilder?" a girl asked.

Damien let go of her hand so fast you'd think it was on fire.

"Yeah. That's me." She smiled.

"Can I *please* have your autograph? I just love you so much."

"Of course!" Sabrina said as she signed the girl's *Teen* magazine. "Thanks for your support."

The Wilder Sisters fans had always been wonderful and supportive. She missed them so much.

"See that?" Damien said when she'd walked away. "It's going to happen a lot more in the future. You're going to hit. Big. All on your own."

That should inspire her, but Sabrina had never wanted to be a superstar. She was just happy singing and performing. Earning just enough money to keep doing it. If hitting big meant she was going to give up the chance at having a private man like Damien in her life, she wasn't sure she liked the idea. But maybe she could have both. Lexi did. Why not her?

"I don't really like L.A.," she admitted as the plane took off. It was smoggy and crowded and not at all like home.

Shades back on, Damien reclined his seat. "Join the club."

"I guess Texas is better?"

"Yeah. It's bigger."

"Damien," she began, lightly touching his forearm.

He tensed, his muscles bunching up under her touch. "I told you to call me D.C. *Everyone* calls me that."

"Everyone but me." She liked his name. Liked the way it rolled over her tongue. D.C. sounded so impersonal.

He sighed. "Sounds about right. I won't let anyone else call me that."

She was quite pleased with this news. "What happens next, when we get back to Whistle Cove?"

"We go to our separate corners."

"I didn't know we had corners."

"You know what I mean." He gazed at her from lowered shades. "I'll make a few phone calls. Get some more label interest. Talk you up. Then we wait."

"What about your cattle ranch?"

"It'll wait."

Seemed that a lot of things waited for this man, and now she would include herself. She would wait for him to realize that a kiss between them would be completely consensual and that he wasn't taking advantage of a single thing.

Tony, Olga's husband and their sometime handyman, picked them up from the airport.

"How was Los Angeles?" Tony asked as he pulled away from the curb.

Damien, who had settled into the front passenger seat alone, probably to better avoid holding her hand, didn't answer. So he was back to his quiet and arrogant self.

"I got to see a lot of touristy things. The Hollywood Walk of Fame. I saw his star, but not the real Denzel Washington."

"The missus will be disappointed," Tony chuckled.

"I brought gifts," she poked through her large carry-on bag. "Tony, I got you a Route 66 T-shirt because you like classic cars so much."

"*Mija*, you didn't have to do that."

"Oh, I know but I wanted to. And I got Olga a calendar with a bunch of movie stars for every month, and I got—"

Damien interrupted. "Mention how we almost missed

our plane because you were shopping for everyone in the world."

"Hey, you took me there!" She pushed on the back of his seat. "How can I leave without something to remember it by?"

It was an hour's drive to Whistle Cove, so when the ocean finally appeared on the right, she was thrilled. Home. The afternoon fog was almost rolling in. She couldn't wait to see Jessie and Gram. It had only been a day but felt like so much longer. So much had happened in a short time that she felt like a new woman. Lighter.

There was something growing between her and Damien that was no longer entirely one-sided. She could sense it in the charged air between them. Like sparks of electricity. Especially when they were alone, but other times, too. She'd catch him studying her with more than a little interest in his dark eyes before he quickly looked away. Maybe he was calculating his risks. Whether he could trust her to be discreet.

She understood far more than he realized. While she believed she could trust him, he couldn't say the same about her. Yet. Considering she would risk far more than he would, his reluctance was tough to understand. He'd soon go to Texas, and she was his last job. Surely his spotless record could be broken once, considering he was retiring.

And even though she wished he'd stick around Whistle Cove after his early retirement, she couldn't think of a single reason for him to stay. And her brain was working overtime to find one.

But there weren't exactly many cattle ranches in the vicinity for this cowboy.

Once they arrived at the B&B, they went separate ways, Damien barely acknowledging her. He thanked Tony, got their bags out, and went to his corner as promised. No "See you later." No "That was fun." Not even a "Hey, sleeping with you was nice."

Sabrina opened the door to her cottage and found Jessie inside.

"Welcome back!" Jessie threw confetti in the air and blew a party horn.

"You're going to clean that up, you know." Sabrina shoulder checked Jessie. "Kidding."

"I missed you, Brina." Jessie used her old family nickname.

"It was one day." Sabrina hugged her sister. Yes, she'd missed her. Missed her conscience. Jessie always gave it to her straight, which meant that she was afraid of what she'd say about the latest development.

"Did you have some fun at least? You didn't spend all the time inside with stuffy executives, did you?"

"Heck, no. We went on a tour bus, and I got to sightsee." She pulled out Jessie's fake Oscar statuette. "For you."

"Aw. Thank you. I always wanted one of these." She turned it in her hands, admiring the gold-plated statue.

"Liar. You wanted a Grammy. We all did." She made her way to the bedroom and opened the French doors to deposit the bags on her bed.

"Hey, we got close."

"Close isn't good enough." She unzipped her garment bag and took out the sparkly dress.

Damien had it dry cleaned by the hotel staff while they'd been on the bus tour and they'd done a great job saving it. She'd never think of this dress in the same way again. It would always remind her of a great evening spent in a hotel room eating room service and watching a movie with Damien. Spooning with him.

"How was D.C.? Still mean and stern?"

"Um, no." She hung the dress up in her closet. "He was actually sweet."

"Sweet?" Jessie made a face, then gasped. "Oh, no. You didn't. Did you *sleep* with him?"

The *sleeping* was a technicality, but she wasn't going to bring it up. Not yet. "You think my sleeping with a man is going to turn him sweet? What a compliment but no. No, I didn't have sex with him. He wouldn't do it."

Jessie went hand to forehead. "What am I going to do with you? Leave the poor man alone. You're probably already making him crazy."

"Poor man? Poor *man*?" Sabrina went hands on hips.

Okay, there was the one tiny incident when even she'd honestly felt bad for him, but she didn't want Jessie to know about that. She would only make more out of it. It had been a mini-meltdown, and now it was over and done. Moving on. Nothing to see here.

"When you get after a man, they're done for. You know, and I know."

"Jessica May Wilder, I've basically had one boyfriend my whole life! One!"

"Sure, but that was only because we traveled so much. But you were the one with all the fan mail and men swearing if you'll just stop in Austin, or Birmingham, or Tallahassee, they'd marry you. You always have men after you, like you're wearing a sign: open for business. Well close it down, Sabrina, close it down!"

"Wow, you're really on a tear today. Ease up on me, yeah?"

"I'm worried about you. D.C. looks like a man who's too *much* man for you to manage if you know what I mean."

Sabrina had been worried about the same thing. She'd

dated boys, or men who behaved like boys, never a real *man*. Especially not one like Damien, who seemed to ooze testosterone from his pores as if he wore it for cologne. Who drank Scotch instead of beer. But she couldn't deny that, after Hollywood, she felt closer to him. She'd thought he felt the same, too, until he really did go to his own corner, as he'd said they should.

"He likes me. He said I'm sexy."

"Oh boy."

"Don't worry. It's not like he'll *do* anything about it. He has ethics and morals and is far too professional. Blah, blah, blah." For once, she had a man she could trust. A man she thought she understood deep down because he was a little bit like her in some ways. He understood scandal and shame. He'd been down and completely remade himself and his future. She admired the man.

A man she wanted more than any man ever before.

"Good thing, too. He's only here a while longer, and then you might never see him again. What's the point in getting intimate just to watch him go?"

"Maybe he'll stay longer. He said we're on Plan B now."

"What, you already ruined Plan A?"

Sabrina scowled. Jessie didn't know anything. "They were encouraging him to use my image as a 'bad girl.' Which is ridiculous. It's not like I had a sex tape. Rise Up wanted to make me an artist with the rock lineup of the label."

Jessie sat on the bed with a plop. "Mom would have a conniption fit."

Sabrina nodded and sat next to her. "She used to say all the rock singers were about sex and drugs all the live long day."

"I think, as usual, she was *exaggerating*."

"I could do without the drugs, but all the sex sounds good."

Jessie did the eye roll thing. "So what happened?"

Sabrina skipped her complete meltdown again. It wouldn't do to rehash the whole thing and she didn't see a purpose in worrying Jessie. "We went to the party, and Damien could tell it wasn't going to work for me, so we're on Plan B."

"Why are you calling him Damien?" Jessie squinted at her.

"Because I can and no one else does."

Jessie rolled her eyes. "Listen, I'll need your help in the morning. Olga's coming in a little late because she has to take Tony to a doctor's appointment. So she has tomorrow's menu set up, and all we need to do is turn on the ovens in the morning and turn them off. Really, it couldn't be easier."

"Do I have to get up at four in the morning?"

"Yes." Jessie deadpanned.

Ah, morning, her evil nemesis. She didn't know if they'd ever be friends. For now they were reluctant acquaintances. "Why not just stick the knife right in my back?"

"You can do this."

"I know."

Didn't mean she had to like it.

9

"Shoot me Straight" by Brothers Osborne

"Jessie, this is hot!" Sabrina jumped back from the oven.

"Use the gloves, Einstein." Jessie threw a pot holder in Sabrina's direction.

"I think twenty minutes was too long to heat the quiche dish up. Now it's going to burn someone's tongue off just like it nearly melted my face when I opened the oven door."

"That's what the directions said. Twenty minutes at 350 degrees."

"I don't think we pay Olga enough," Sabrina said, moving the baked dish to the counter to join the others.

"How do *you* know how much we pay her?"

She shook her head. "Whatever it is can't be enough."

"And I used to think that getting all hot and sweaty playing the drums two hours a night was hard work," Jessie said.

Four o'clock in the freaking morning. No one was up at this time, not even the sun! Even Damien would probably be sleeping. She wondered if he usually slept naked. Sabrina shook her head, trying to lose the lustful thought. She fully planned on catching him in the act of jogging on the beach since Jessie said he seemed to do that every morning. If Sabrina had to be up this early, she would enjoy the view. She'd staked her position on the wrap-around deck with the best view of their private beach and all the nutty joggers.

A couple of hours later, and the buffet set-up complete, guests began to arrive, going straight for the coffee machine. Sabrina was on her fourth cup of the brown liquid, so she could relate. Coffee was even beginning to taste better, and she understood the compulsion that most of the population had with it. Coffee served its purpose. Plus, it was warm and not terrible if you added plenty of sugar and cream.

After the food was heated and served, they only had to replace the hot serving dishes with new filled ones when they got close to empty. Finally, when the last tray was out, Sabrina made her way to the outside deck. She chatted with guests who wanted directions to the Monterey Bay Aquarium. Another wanted directions to Cannery Row. Still another couple wanted to share all their plans for their fiftieth wedding anniversary celebration. She listened patiently, wondering how two people put up with each other for that many years.

The morning was cool and quiet. Calm. The sun had come up in its usual way, not making a big fuss as it hid behind a cloud. The seagulls were doing their thing: crying and flying while the waves rolled in and out. Sabrina eyed Damien jogging down the beach in her direction at a slow and even pace ahead of the other joggers. She waved. He didn't wave back, but he slowed and made his way up the winding wooden steps to the deck. Her heart raced as he got closer, and she forgot what she was going to say.

"Morning, Sunshine. What are you doing up so early?"

The man didn't even look out of breath after all that running. Impressive. "Um, I had to help Jessie with breakfast. Olga's got the day off."

He took a seat at an empty wrought-iron table. "Never asked. What do you usually do around here?"

"A little bit of everything. My grandmother used to be the innkeeper here with my grandfather Wilder. They used to manage and do it all. Now we've got a great cook and a handyman, but even so, Jessie pretty much manages the place. All I do is wash, dry and fold towels and sheets, clean some of the rooms, pour coffee and wine, socialize during wine tasting hour." She numbered them off one by one with her fingers.

Another thing she only did when she was nervous because Damien had her sweating, and she didn't quite know why. Pretty soon she'd make a joke, but right now she had nothing. Her mind was empty of every thought that didn't involve what he looked like in the morning. Unshaven, hair mussed when he normally never had a single hair out of place. And he looked so sexy in his board shorts and a sweatshirt that read *Dallas Cowboys*.

"Um, you should probably not wear that around here." She pointed to his shirt and went for a nervous laugh. "This is 49er territory. You could be crucified, mind you."

"I'll take my chances." He smirked.

"Can I get you anything?" She flew into hospitality mode. "Coffee, tea…"

Me? Lame, Sabrina. Lame.

He raised brows as if he'd read her mind. "Coffee, black. No sugar."

"Be right back." Who took their coffee black with no sugar? It had to taste like death that way.

She poured him a mug, then loaded a plate with the hot dish and a blueberry muffin. Olga's pastries were award-winning. These muffins had large chunks of blueberries in them and the cake was melt-in-your-mouth buttery and soft. She struggled to manage both in her hands since she'd never been a waitress. Not even close.

When she set it down in front of him she actually got a grin. "Such service."

"Enjoy your breakfast. Olga's muffins won an award last year at the Monterey Bake-off, you know. She's won awards before, of course. It wasn't the first time." Before her rambling went into overdrive, she stopped herself. "Okay. I'll see you."

"Wait. You busy now?"

All that waited was sheets and towels, Lexi's old job. Jessie basically ran the B&B, but Sabrina and Lexi had helped where they could. When the Wilder Sisters had come off the hamster wheel of life on the road, they'd come home to Whistle Cove to help their paternal grandmother.

And hide from the media, too.

"Just making the rounds, welcoming and chatting with all our guests. Seeing how I can help Jessie."

"Sit down with me," he ordered. "I'm a guest."

It wasn't a request, but she did so easily, hoping they were going to give up their corners. "What's up?"

"Tell me about yourself."

"What do you want to know?"

"Things I can't learn by doing a simple internet search. What do you really want out of life?" He took a swallow of his coffee and studied her from under hooded eyelids.

Good, they were starting with the easy questions first.

She cleared her throat and squirmed in her seat. Had anyone actually asked her that? Ever? She'd been put on a stage at the age of ten, when her daddy claimed that she was a born performer, Lexi a natural at writing songs, and Jessie the kind of supportive sister who would do anything asked of her, including play the drums. And yes, Sabrina had loved her old life. Loved traveling with her sisters and parents, singing and performing.

It's just that no one had *ever* asked.

She wondered why no one had asked. Because it might have been nice to go to the prom instead of practicing every weekend. Now here was this man who barely knew her, and he wanted to know what made her tick.

"I...I..." she began. Dear God, why wasn't this easier?

Remind him you want to get back to Nashville. Back to singing and performing. Back to a more public life. It was invasive and all consuming, but she loved it, too. Probably. Mostly.

"Take your time." He set the mug down and took a bite of the muffin.

She drummed her fingers on the table. "You know, no one has ever asked me that."

"Do you know?" he asked, and it didn't seem to be a question meant to irritate her. There was simple curiosity in his words.

"Of course," she said. "I want to get back to singing and performing."

"And that's it?"

Why did this feel like a test, and she was underperforming? "Isn't that enough?"

No, no, it isn't. Too bad she couldn't articulate what was missing from the equation. She'd start off with the need for a man in her life, sex, and real companionship, but that sounded so shallow. And she knew she wanted more. Far more. The past year had been a forced introspection, and she'd looked at her life for the first time and the choices she'd made. There weren't many.

But the worst had been the way she'd trusted a man she'd barely known, simply because she'd been lonely. Had she been more penitent about her mistake at the start, maybe the whole thing wouldn't have been much of a story. Granted, there were far more salacious scandals going on, but she'd been known for her clean and wholesome image. The media ate up the story of the wholesome girl gone wild.

Lexi had been the first to admit that the blowing up of their band and the forced time off had been a welcome break. For Sabrina, it had been entirely different. The guilt she'd felt knowing she'd been the cause of plummeting sales, and eventually being dropped from the label, had stuck with her. Even when her sisters had rallied around her. Even when Mama and Gran had forgiven her naiveté and assured her that Daddy would have forgiven her too.

The boulder that had been dropped on her heart and guilty conscience had eased off slowly. Recently, she'd been trying to think about what her life might look like from this point forward. Before Lexi had returned to Nashville, and thus almost ensured that Sabrina would eventually follow, she had briefly wondered if there might be something else for her to do. If there was, she hadn't found it. But it seemed that maybe she should want to find something else. Somewhere she could make a difference in the world. Though it probably wasn't running a B&B.

"For some people, sure," Damien said. "It would be enough."

"I don't know why you're asking me all this. Why do you care, anyway?"

"Because no one has asked you this before. That's why I care."

"If you care so much, why not meet me later in my cottage and I'll *show* you what I want," she teased. Flirting. Joking. Something she understood.

He didn't bite. "That's your defensive posture, you know?"

"Flirting?"

"Sex."

Well, hell, she didn't know she would get psychoanalyzed by the so-called fixer. "Is this part of the service you provide? Shrinking my head?"

He gave her his scary calm again. "Just think of it as a bonus."

"I don't really want to talk about any of this right now."

"Too bad."

"You're so annoying!"

"Right back at ya," he said, taking a sip of his coffee. "Here's the thing. You remind me of myself. When I was seventeen and couldn't think about anything but sex."

Ouch! Her cheeks burned so hot it was almost painful. "Yeah? Tell me, were you having a lot of sex when you were seventeen?"

"No. Wasn't. That's kind of the point."

She crossed her arms. "What is?"

"A person tends to think a lot about sex when it feels like everyone else is having it but them," he said. "I'm going to tell you what my football coach told me. *Mind over matter.*"

She was getting lessons on abstinence from *this* guy? Seriously? Because she had news for him: her middle name might as well be Abstinence. That's where she'd gotten into all of the trouble. Unrealistic expectations.

She'd never signed up for that. "This is a nice redirect.

Are you going to keep denying that we have something between us? *You* think I'm sexy."

"Not denying a damn thing. I'm telling you: mind over matter, Sunshine. Mind over matter." He stood. "I'm taking the high road. Care to join me up here?"

She pressed her lips together. He was right, damn him. This wasn't about the two of them and whatever sparks they had between them that threatened to ignite the coastline. She had to get her head on straight. He'd been hired to help resuscitate a career on life-support. A career and a life she wanted back because it was all she knew.

"I'm joining you on that high road. Move on over."

Mind over matter.

Thank you, Coach Lyons. The mantra had gotten D.C. through high school varsity with all his efforts gaining him a scholarship to take him out of his small East Texas town. Now it would get him through the roadblock named Sabrina Wilder, a woman who'd staged a *coup d'état* on his hormones. Ever since he'd stirred awake in the middle of the night to find her, sound asleep, her back to him, wearing nothing but that tee, he hadn't been the same. She was more beautiful than he'd realized. Smooth, creamy skin and full sensual lips. She had a sweet arousing smell that was all her own. But with Sabrina, it wasn't just her looks. Yes, she was blonde and curvy but that wasn't it.

She *did* things to him. Made him feel the kind of desire and pull for a woman that he hadn't felt in years. It had been almost instinctive to pull her back to him and keep his arms tight around her. He hadn't meant to do it all night long. He'd meant to get up after a few minutes, go back to his room and his own bed. Next thing he knew, he'd spent the whole night with her. And nothing had happened. He hadn't known he possessed that kind of self-control. Should have nudged her awake and given her what she'd been asking from him since almost the moment they'd met.

She didn't know it, but the two of them were too much alike. Prone to emotion. Reckless. He'd learned the tough way to control his instincts. But she was the kind of woman the word "trouble" had been invented for, and he had to stay away. There was no room for her in his life and no room for him in hers. She wouldn't be happy on his ranch, and he couldn't be happy being "Mr. Wilder", following her tour bus and watching the world (and men) fawn all over her. If that made him sound unsupportive, he was. He didn't like show business. He wanted to fade into the background the moment he arrived on his cattle ranch. Live a simple and uncomplicated life. But now Sabrina had him wanting all kind of other things, too. Like someone warming his bed every night.

Damn!

This morning after his run, he'd ignored the way his heart rate kicked up at the sight of her standing on the deck, waving to him. Told himself to shut it down. Stop indulging her before it got out of control. He no longer cared about his spotless record, and that scared the crap out of him. He *should* care, looming retirement or not. So, he reminded himself again and again of Coach Lyons' mantra. And he would be repeating it to himself often the next week.

The high road. Yes sir, he would be taking it.

As he made his way back to his room, the phone buzzed, and he pulled it out of his pocket. "Caldwell."

"Checking in. The offer went in as planned, but there's

still no response. I'm bugging their agent daily," said Annie King, his real estate agent in Texas.

"Is that normal?" He'd purchased and flipped plenty of real estate in the past, but never a property for personal use. Rules and standards were different, he understood.

"Not usually, though this is a huge exchange. It may take time to get through all the brokers. Would you consider making an offer on any of the other ranches we looked at?"

A couple of months ago, marshaling all of his resources, he'd toured all the ranches for sale in Texas. There were many that had trouble, unable to sustain operations. He'd buy all of them if he could. Instead he'd settled on the second largest cattle ranch in Texas in a town called Juniper three hours outside Dallas. In that part of Texas, family ties ran deep. The Farrells were overextended with liens on their property. But with a working cattle ranch that was at least self-sustaining, the Farrells could afford to ask full price. They'd likely get plenty of offers.

"I want *this* ranch," he said.

"Are you sure? I'm only reminding you, but with what you're paying for this cattle ranch, you could almost have two smaller ones. Or buy a modern mansion. Twelve-car garage, tennis courts, swimming pool."

"Not interested."

She'd been asking this since he'd hired her, and he was growing tired of it. He had his reasons for wanting the ranch. If he bought a mansion, what would he do all day? Stare at the TV? Count his garages? She'd suggested entertaining, but he was burnt-out on galas and parties. He was only thirty-two, so he wasn't retiring from life, simply from the career that had enabled him to acquire all his wealth.

From the time he'd been a kid until he'd found football, horses and the rodeo had been his life. When he'd discovered after his mother's death that his father was Conrad Caldwell, of the *Texas* Caldwells, owner of the largest cattle ranch in the state, suddenly everything fell into place.

Ranching was in his blood as much as football had ever been. He'd gone to college on his own, requiring no help from the senior Caldwell, who'd never given his mother a dime. After he'd knocked her up and refused to marry her, she'd never asked him for a thing, though she'd given Damien the Caldwell last name. His mother might not have demanded anything from Conrad, but D.C. sure in the hell did.

He'd gone to his father after losing his scholarship, just shown up to his sprawling ranch compound unannounced and demanded to be recognized. In exchange for never asking for a DNA test or revealing his identity to the rest of his family, Conrad had given D.C. a generous settlement.

Ironically, since most of their negotiations had taken place with the man Conrad used to "fix" his problems, D.C. had himself an unintentional mentor. Now, years after his first meeting with Conrad, D.C. would soon own the second largest ranch in Texas. Eventually, he hoped it would grow to be the largest.

Anything to put the old man in his place.

10

"Five More Minutes" by Scotty McCreery

D.C. had first become acquainted with the Wilder Sisters when he'd met Lexi Wilder and her fiancé Luke Wyatt in Nashville. As a bright and shiny power couple the media was itching to pursue, they'd needed help navigating their very public life. He'd helped, they'd thanked him, and he'd moved on. A week or two later, a call had come in from Luke, asking if he'd help Lexi's little sister, so-called instigator of the mini-scandal. He called it a mini-scandal because he'd dealt with far worse.

He'd agreed to take the job and make it his last one. A way to go out on a good note. Easy job. And quite honestly, he'd felt for the family. Traveling around Nashville circles from time to time, he'd met John Wilder before his unfortunate passing. A good and honest man, John had never required D.C.'s services, but he'd known plenty of stars who had. Referred D.C. to a couple of them.

Wonder what he'd think about his youngest daughter needing D.C.'s services? D.C was only guessing, but he believed the thoughts would run parallel to his own: find the man-child who'd sold the photo to the media in the first place. Teach *him* a lesson. But D.C. wasn't reckless anymore. That was the old him. The new and improved Damien Caldwell glossed over the cause of the trouble, ran a Hail Mary pass right over it, and went straight to solving the issue at hand. No point in wasting time over what could not be changed.

Despite all that, if he ever met the guy in a dark alley, all bets were off.

For his homework, he'd watched old recorded performances of the Wilder Sisters. Sabrina had been the consummate performer, as easy on a stage as if she'd been born on one. She'd commanded every song with a strong and sensual voice. With choreographed sexy moves that made any grown man pay attention. He'd admired the ease with which she worked the crowd. A skill he'd had to learn the hard way came naturally to her. He envied that on some level. She didn't have to fake it. Sabrina loved people, and the people loved her. It was hard not to.

Today, he'd spent the day making phone calls and networking on Sabrina's behalf. There was already interest at the largest record label in Nashville. His goal was to have multiple labels interested in her staging a comeback. It would have to be Nashville, the only way she'd be happy. With her sister writing her a song or two, the road was already paved. All he had to do was show them she was ready to return to public life. Demonstrate she wouldn't have a public meltdown if asked again about the photo. For that, he only had a few lessons left to give her on fame. At that point, it would be up to her and whether she was only doing this because it was all she knew.

He had news for her: football had once been his entire

future. These days, he was simply a die-hard fan. Sabrina
had to decide for herself if she was going to keep that presence and charisma she owned hiding under a blanket, or if
she would share it with the world. After talking with her
this morning, he had the unnerving impression that she
wasn't entirely sure. At least, not for the right reasons. And
she would have to be certain. Another stupid mistake or
miscalculation on her part and this comeback wouldn't be
smooth. He never left a job undone.

Tired of living in his bedroom, comfortable though it
was with the king-sized bed and clawfoot tub in the bathroom, he decided to join their wine tasting hour. He'd
turned into a reluctant but necessary connoisseur of wine
over the years, and he knew his grapes. There was a small
group of people downstairs, mostly consisting of couples,
sitting on the couches and chairs. Engaged in conversations.
Flirting. Touching. Like most B&Bs it was much like walking
into someone's living room. The stone fireplace flickered
with flames on this September night, appropriate for the
foggy, cool weather. Couples were wandering outside onto
the private beach, most wearing sweaters and long pants.

Sabrina, sipping from a glass of red wine, was engaged
in conversation with an older couple. Her eyes brightened
when she caught sight of him. Taking care to tamp down the
adrenaline that coursed through him at seeing her, he
picked up and inspected a bottle of Cabernet Sauvignon.
California, naturally. Not a bad year. He poured a small
amount in a glass and watched it swirl around the bottom.
Noted its properties. Got distracted by the sound of Sabrina's wicked and rich belly laugh. That girl could make
simple laughter sound like a proposition.

"Do you know much about wines?" A woman had come

up to his side. She looked to be in her late forties and had short dark hair and earnest blue eyes.

"Took a few classes." He let the wine breathe and settle.

"A man after my own heart. Not too proud to learn something new. Well, good for you!"

"It helped with my work." Not everyone drank good Scotch, and when the Scotch was piss poor, a good wine would do. Becoming adept at understanding wine had helped him land a client who was in the vineyard business... until his gambling got out of control. He'd almost lost everything.

That one had been a difficult job. One of his earliest.

"What do you do?" The woman asked.

He got ready to do some creative framing, one of his specialties. "I work with struggling companies and bring them back to their former value."

"Like for the stock market?"

"Something like that." He took a sip of wine.

"I'm Molly, by the way." She offered her hand.

"D.C." He shook her hand.

"What an interesting name. I'm a good friend of Kit's."

"Is she around?" He scanned the room. With no idea how well she'd aged from the few photos of her he'd seen, he had no idea if he could find Kit Wilder in a crowd.

"Hi, Molly," Sabrina interrupted. "I didn't see you."

"I just dropped off a flower delivery and thought I'd say hello to you all." Molly rather boldly squeezed his forearm.

"Molly runs the only flower shop in town," Sabrina explained, zeroing in on his covered arm.

"And Kit and I go way back," Molly said, not letting go of him.

"That's true," Sabrina said and, with eyes that could pass

for lasers, stared at Molly's hand until she reluctantly removed it.

He shook his head at the unnerving feeling that Sabrina had just claimed him. Not sure how he felt about that.

Molly sighed. "Well, I'm off!"

"Bye, Molly. I'll tell Mom you dropped by."

"Nice to meet you," D.C. said.

"You as well, D.C." She waved as she walked away.

"You can thank me later," Sabrina said as they watched Molly walk away. "She's a cougar."

"Yeah?" He casually glanced back to the woman's retreating form. "Interesting. Why did you chase her away?"

"She likes younger men," Sabrina pressed, as if he was a clueless guy. "She was interested in you. She wanted to...*you* know."

He squinted. "And what's wrong with that?"

"Um, well, nothing really. I just thought you...I mean because of...I didn't want her to..."

"Take it easy, Sunshine." It was difficult not to laugh. "I'm teasing you."

"Oh," she said, and her shoulders sagged. Recovering quickly, she slapped his chest. "Cut it out."

"Teasing you?"

"Yeah, that!" She pointed at him.

"But it's fun." He set his wine glass down.

Her shimmering green eyes met his, a smile tugging at the corners of her sweet lips. This was her wheelhouse. She enjoyed playing with him, and now he was tangling with her. No idea why.

"Did you like the wine?" she asked.

"Kind of earthy with a fruity undertone. I'm guessing apricot."

She gaped at him. "Yeah?"

"I took a class. No big deal."

"What are you doing down here, anyway?"

"Decided to come check this out." He tipped his chin in the direction of the room. "And now I have. Think I'm going to take a walk."

"That's a good idea. I would normally suggest that to our guests. It's a nice night. Not too cold."

"Don't lie. It's freezing out there."

"Not for natives." She gave him a smile.

"I'm from Texas."

"I know. You're a cowboy at heart."

She had him pegged, didn't she? Pleasure rolled through him at her simple but true statement. Not everyone saw him for who he truly was. Most of his close friends had thought the cattle ranch was a crazy idea from a man with too much money.

"Yeah, well, this cowboy is going for a walk without his horse."

"...AND so, twenty years later, here we are again," the woman concluded.

Was her name Irene? No. Rayleen, or...Sabrina was so bad with names. A face she never forgot. She could say with certainty she'd never seen this couple before.

"She wouldn't remember, Eileen. She's just a baby," the woman's husband said.

Eileen! Sabrina had been speaking to the sixty-some-thing couple ever since D.C. had left the room. She wanted to join him, because, after all he was a guest as well, and she should be attentive. But just seconds from a clean getaway she'd been pulled into a conversation with the couple. They were nice people visiting all the way from Missouri because they'd met twenty years ago on a nature hike organized by the town of Whistle Cove.

"No, she doesn't remember," Eileen said. "She must have been, what, eight?"

"Six." And four years away from headlining a family band. "But my sisters and I would sometimes hang out here on the weekend."

"Well, after those first few days, we spent most of the time in a bedroom, so she wouldn't have seen much of us anyway," the man said.

"Jeff!" Eileen covered her mouth.

Jeff lifted a shoulder and grinned. "She's old enough to know."

"All these years, we had no idea the Wilder Sisters B&B and the Wilder Sisters act was the same family! We loved watching you girls play and listening to your songs. Any chance you'll be back on the stage anytime soon?"

"Babe," Jeff said. "We've monopolized her time long enough."

"I'm sorry, dear," Eileen said. "I'm talking your ear off."

"You never know, there might be a certain man you're keeping her from," Jeff said.

"Well...," Sabrina began.

"There is!" Eileen said and pointed to her eyes. "I can tell. You've got that sparkle in your eye."

Sparkle? She had a sparkle in her eye? Which eye? She didn't know about her eyes, but there was something definitely going on with the rest of her body. It wasn't a spark, but more like an electrical current pulling her toward Damien.

Jeff took Eileen's hand and tugged her to him. "If you'll excuse me, I'm going to take my wife on a nature walk."

But they headed in the direction of the rooms, their arms wrapped around each other.

Sweet. Sabrina's parents had been that loving, and she had no doubt they'd still be were her daddy still alive. They'd been the couple who danced together in the kitchen. The couple who never tired of each other or of being together.

Her parents had wanted the same things from life and worked together in a perfect partnership. Having witnessed such an example of love and devotion, Sabrina had such a high bar to meet that she sometimes doubted she'd ever reach it.

Lexi had been fortunate enough to wind up with her first love, and Luke was also a musician, so they had everything in common. But Sabrina kept being attracted to men with whom she had nothing in common. Like Damien. This time was notably different. She'd always been attracted to strong, athletic, muscular men. That was nothing new.

With him, far more than his looks drew her to him. It was the way he challenged her like few people in her life ever had, without backing down once. That, coupled with the tender side of him she'd now seen firsthand, officially made him the kind of man she'd never met before.

Stopping briefly to say hello to Gran and her gentleman friend, Sir Clint, on her way out, Sabrina then headed to the beach to find a certain cowboy. As long as he would be in Whistle Cove and helping her career, she wanted to know more about him. She found him not far down the private access beach, his back to her, hands shoved in his pockets. The sun had begun its slow slide, a beautiful red splash of color meeting the deep blue horizon of the sea.

"Hey," she said from behind him. "Here you are."

He turned and met her eyes, acknowledging her presence, but then turned back to the sunset without a single word.

Definitely the quiet type.

She came to his side, but when he continued to remain calm and stoic beside her, she got nervous. Antsy. There were two things she often did when nervous: make a joke or start singing. Granted, she didn't just sing when she was nervous. She also sang when she was bored, sad, happy, in the shower, not in the shower, on the beach alone, on the beach with her sisters, and...okay, pretty much always.

Now, she sang under her breath softly so as not to interrupt his quiet time. It was just a little something she was playing around with in her head. She'd never written a single song of her own because Lexi always had one ready for her. But many times, she played around in her head with a tune and words which were always difficult to pull out of thin air. She hadn't been singing long when Damien turned to her, a smile tugging at the corners of his lips.

"What?" she asked, stopping.

"Nothing," he said, facing her now. "Keep going, but louder."

"Oh, ha, ha. I get it. No, that's not really a song." She tucked a chunk of her wind-blown hair behind her ear.

"What is it?"

"Well...it's...I guess it's the start of a song?"

"You don't know?" Now his lips were full on tipped up in a smile.

"It *is* the start of a song. But it's not much, so I don't want to sing louder if you don't mind."

"I don't." He took a step toward her. "What are you doing out here?"

"I-I came to find you. You said you're not used to this kind of weather, and—"

"You're scared for me." Another slow, easy smile.

She shook her head. The wind had kicked up, and her hair was doing its crazy thing, flying around her head like straw. "Don't be silly. I know you can take care of yourself."

"Yeah? You said I was afraid. Because you could rock my world."

A strangled laugh came out of her. Sometimes she wished she could buy a leash for her tongue. She talked too much sometimes. Or all the time. "That was before. When you were being annoying and all."

"And now? I'm not being annoying anymore?" He reached to tuck a flyaway hair behind her ear, then his fingers wandered to her chin.

"You were really sweet to me in Hollywood."

"Right. Don't get used to that. That's not who I am."

Clearly, it wasn't who he wanted to be. She got the message. "Okay, then, who are you?"

His fingers traced her lips, and she began to lose focus on the conversation. "I'm a man who doesn't get attached. I don't fall in love. I don't make plans or commitments. When something isn't working, I walk away. It's that easy."

She tried to smile. "Wow. So, what you're telling me is that you're a romantic."

"No." He didn't laugh. "But you're a tease who likes to play with fire."

It pissed her off when people called her out on her shit. This man was very good at it. No wonder he'd pushed all of her buttons since day one.

Since his finger was still on her lower lip, she nipped it. "I'm not teasing."

There was a flash of surprise in his eyes, gone too quickly, and then his eyes darkened with heat. She returned fire, meeting his gaze, unable to break away. Unwilling to back down. Not when she knew exactly what she wanted. The rest of her life might be in a state of chaos, but in this small moment, she wanted only one thing. It was him.

"Stop," he ordered. "I can't hurt you."

"You won't. You know what I've been through. I don't scare easily anymore."

"And I doubt you ever did." One arm hooked her by the waist and suddenly she was flat against him.

Her hands skimmed from his forearms to his biceps, and then she wrapped her arms around his neck. She tipped on the balls of her feet, stared at his mouth, and willed him to do it now. Kiss her and end the mystery. Because she was dying here. When he didn't, but simply continued to eat her alive with his gaze, she pressed him. Reminded him. Handed him the invitation.

"This is what we both want."

11

"Kiss Somebody" by Morgan Evans

Fortunately for Sabrina, those seemed to be the words Damien needed from her. He took the cue and bent to take her mouth in a scorching kiss. But scorching wasn't the right word. Sweltering. Steamy. Unbelievably hot. He wasn't tender, but he was demanding. Pressing her even closer to him, hands on her behind, he tugged her to him as intimately as two people could be without taking their clothes off. And still it wasn't enough. She wanted to climb him like a rock, rip his clothes off, and let him inside. For a moment he pulled back, his hand on the nape of her neck, controlling her every movement. Surprise registered in his eyes again, but this time it stayed.

He went back to kissing her again and again, sinking his fingers in her hair and angling her head where he wanted it to be, plunging his tongue inside deeper. When he stopped a few minutes, or a few hours later, they were both out of breath. She'd known it would be like this between them. Combustive. Explosive.

She'd realized from the moment she'd laid eyes on him that he'd change her forever. She just didn't know how. Her body felt as if it was on fire from the inside out, and a sharp tingle of anticipation spiked down her thighs. She wondered if he felt this intensity, too. If she was to go by the way he continued to hold her tightly against him, he might feel the same way.

"You're surprised," she whispered when he broke the kiss. When she could formulate words again.

"Yeah," he said on a ragged breath.

"I'm not. I knew it would be like this with us." She heard guests approaching and buried her face in his neck.

"We should go inside," he said, reading her mind.

He didn't wait for her to agree but pulled her in the direction of her cottage. Yes, this was a good idea. Her cottage, so that Jessie wouldn't see them and have a million and one questions. Questions Sabrina didn't want to answer. Also, best that Gran not see them together and make a judgment about Damien.

She didn't want anyone judging *him* because this had been her idea. If he was on board now, it was because he'd accidentally found she'd been right about them all along. Now he wanted her too, and that knowledge slipped through her like a soft and light caress.

"You remember what I told you, Sunshine?" he asked in a rich and deeply sensual voice.

"I know. You don't do love."

She repeated the words he'd said so she could hear them out loud again. She would remember not to get attached. Would remember not to let this moment, however wonderful it turned out to be, derail her life. She had plans to make that wouldn't include him. But right now, she had him and he was unlike anyone she'd ever known. Her hand shook as she opened the door to her home, his body heat sweltering from where he stood behind her.

"And you should know," she said. "I don't usually do this. I know my reputation, but I'm a good girl."

"I know." His warm breath tickled her neck. "That's why I tried to stay away."

They weren't in the house with the door shut two minutes when he had her up against the door, arms pinned above her head, ravaging her with open-mouth kisses. Lips, neck, earlobes. Nothing escaped the warmth of his mouth and tongue. If he kept this up, they'd do it right here, right now, like this. She was ready when he released her arms because then she could touch him like she'd been dying to do. She could let her fingers drift under his shirt and over his tense abs. But when he knelt in front of her that became difficult to do. She watched as he unzipped her jeans and lowered them, wondering if they were really about to have sex up against a door.

"I have...a...a...," she said as he pulled her panties down to her ankles.

But then he groaned and put his mouth on her, his tongue licking every intimate tender part, and she forgot to remind him that she had a perfectly good bed. With every one of his movements it seemed as if he was familiar with her and knew exactly what to do without being told.

"Open for me," he ordered and spread her legs apart with his shoulders.

She helped, wanting badly to please him, though the position was awkward. But when he continued to tease her mercilessly, she had other problems. She was certain her skin was tight enough to split her into a million pieces. Just when she couldn't take any more pleasure, wiggling and shaking, she crested a powerful peak and cried out, digging fingernails into his shoulders. He kept her from hitting the ground as her legs gave way.

Then he slung her over his shoulder. "Bed."

"Yes," she agreed, viewing the world upside down and not minding it one bit.

The French doors to her room were already opened as she'd left them, and he laid her gently on the bed. She pulled her jeans off the rest of the way, along with her panties, and tossed them aside. About to take her sweater off, she stopped everything when she noticed what Damien was doing. Her breath caught in her throat. He was taking his shirt off, and this she did not want to miss even for the second it would take to yank her top off.

She gaped, unable to look away, as he tossed the button-up shirt to the side and went for his pants. His arms were thick and brawny. A striking tribal tattoo below his pec wound around to his back. It was interesting, but there were other stimulating things going on. Such as Damien stepping out of his jeans to reveal sinewy thighs and so much more. None of him disappointed. He was big and beautiful, and for now he was all hers.

All.

Hers.

"Are you done?" he asked, jerking her out of her daze. He was smirking.

Oh, crap, mental face plant. She was staring at his body as if hypnotized. How embarrassing. It was almost as if she'd never seen a naked man before. Well, she'd never seen one that looked like *this*. Not in person.

She ducked her head to tug off her sweater, which accomplished being able to hide her flushed face for a second. "Um, I was just wondering if this is what all cowboys look like under their chaps. Because I think I've been missing out."

He snorted. "It's my turn now. I want to see all of you."

She unsnapped and slipped off her bra, and then was completely bared to him. Lying back on the bed, she let him take his fill of her as she had with him. She didn't feel self-conscious or shy with him which surprised her. Her body wasn't perfect.

She didn't like to work out unless it was on a stage. There was also her long-running love affair with potato chips. But he didn't seem to notice any extra flesh. His heated gaze skimmed over her body, hungry with desire, and everywhere he landed she nearly burned with the heat.

"Fuck. You are so beautiful."

Covering her with his body, his fingers skimmed her breast and tweaked a nipple. Everywhere he touched, he followed with his warm tongue. He pulled her nipple into his mouth and sucked hard. Her back arched with pleasure and heat pooled between her legs. He worked her like that, bringing her close to orgasm but then pulling back. It was sweet, sweet agony.

After an interminable time, she was desperate to have him inside her and clawed at his rigid butt. "Please, Damien."

"Are you ready for me?" One finger dipped inside her and gave him the evidence he needed. "Yeah."

It was only then that she remembered they needed protection. Optimistic though she'd been, she wasn't prepared for *this* to happen tonight. And despite her current reputation, she hadn't been with a man in years.

"I don't...have anything here," she said on a hoarse breath.

An expression she couldn't read flashed in his eyes, and he reached for his wallet. "I've got it."

Her curiosity piqued, she wondered if the condom could be expired. "Is it an old one?"

"No," he said, not looking at her. "I bought some a couple of nights ago."

"A couple of *nights* ago?"

Delight shot through her when she registered that he'd wanted her enough to plan for this moment. Enough to drive to the drugstore and spend money on something he'd hoped he would need. Talk about optimistic. Oh, who was she kidding? He'd simply been realistic. She'd wanted him from Day One, even when he'd annoyed the living hell out of her.

"Don't look so surprised. After sleeping next to you, I knew I would never survive another night like that without having you."

Speechless, she watched as he ripped the packet open and slowly covered himself. It was such a turn-on that she nearly came again without him. Then his hard body was on top of hers again, kissing her everywhere with his soul-branding tongue. He spread her legs and with one long stroke was deep inside of her, making them both moan.

Moments later, his strokes became tentative. Slow. "You okay?"

"Y-yes."

He felt it, too. Because he was large, and he stretched her. But it didn't hurt at all. Instead it seemed as if this place inside her was ready and waiting to be filled. She needed him. She was ready for him. Placing her hands on his butt, she urged him on. He obliged eagerly, and his thrusts went deeper and harder, taking her to a place of powerful pleasure like she'd never known before.

She'd liked sex the few times she'd had it, but this. This was different. It was more than sex. More...everything. Every one of her senses was engaged as she touched him, tasted him, heard his ragged breaths, and smelled his earthy, manly scent.

He moved inside her longer than she would have believed possible, and the entire time he kept a tight control she couldn't understand. She was falling apart here, and he was measured. Completely together. And then she realized he was waiting for her.

The knowledge of that kindness was the last seam to rip, and she flew apart for him moments later, coming in gasps and moans that sounded like they'd come out of a stranger. She got to watch him, then, as he also let go, cursing and groaning her name.

Taking his weight off her, he braced himself above her and simply studied her for several minutes. She was certain he was just as surprised as her. He tucked her next to him, and she curled one leg over his. Both of them were quiet for a few moments, and she wondered if he was thinking the same thing. This couldn't just be a one-time thing. She wouldn't let it be.

"We have a problem, Sunshine," he said, his fingers gently caressing the nape of her neck.

Oh no. This was where he told her that they'd go back to their corners after tonight. This was where he dropped her because he'd gotten what he wanted from her.

"We do?" she whispered, almost afraid to hear the answer.

"Yeah," he said, his voice deep and gruff. "I don't know if I can get enough of you."

"Really?" She lifted her head from his chest to look at him. Her heart gave a powerful tug.

He nodded, looking somber, as if he didn't really like the fact.

He'd told her that he didn't fall in love. She reminded herself that sex and love were different for men. Easy to separate. He didn't mean he could *fall in love* with her. He meant he wanted more sex. She didn't disagree with that point.

"Admit it. I'm damn good in bed. You want more." She *had* to joke.

"That's too easy to admit."

"It's not just you who wants another go at this."

"That's good to hear, because you're addictive for me." His hands skimmed down her spine and came to rest at the small of her back. "But you remember what I said."

"I sure do. That doesn't mean you have to keep repeating it." She flicked his pec with her finger.

"Sorry. But I don't want to hurt you or take advantage."

"Yes, you've said that like a million times." She disentangled and climbed over him to get out of bed. "I've got something for you."

She'd bought it at the gift shop in Hollywood even while he complained that she would make them lose their flight. But then he'd gone to his corner, and she'd doubted he deserved her thoughtful gift. He certainly did now. She pulled it out of her dresser drawer, crawled back into bed, and handed him the wrapped tissue paper.

"What's this?" he asked, taking it from her.

"Remember when you were complaining I would make us miss our flight? Then you went outside to wait because you couldn't take it anymore?"

"Yeah," he said slowly and suspiciously.

"I got this for you." She bounced on the bed. "I can't

believe you haven't unwrapped it yet. If it were me, I'd have torn into it in two seconds."

He gave her a slow smile, then tore off the paper to reveal a silver-plated western style belt buckle with the word *Hollywood* imprinted on the front.

"It's got a little bit of everything. Cowboy and Hollywood. It's both tacky and traditional. And I thought you might like to remember me when you got back to Texas and all your cowboy ways."

"You realize I won't ever wear this?" He turned it over in his hands.

"Aw," she said with mock disappointment.

"But I'll always keep it." He set it aside then reached to pull her into his arms. "Believe that."

She buried her face in his warm neck. "Damien, you do realize I've been a willing participant here all along. Don't feel guilty about us."

"This just seems too good to be true, so excuse me if I'm suspicious."

She sat up straight. "Oh, so now I'm too good to be true? I'm going to need to take out an ad. I'll have the men lining up for a chance with that kind of an endorsement."

He scowled. "Don't even think about it. While I'm here, I'm not sharing you with anyone else. Not your ex, not a fan. Not a friend. No one."

"The same goes for me, you know."

"You're not talking about Molly." His eyes narrowed.

"Why not? She had her *hand* on your forearm. She wants you."

"Yeah, she had her hand on my arm. In some cultures that means we're engaged." He smirked.

"Okay, smartass. But don't say I didn't warn you." She lightly smacked his chest.

He chuckled. "I think you're jealous."

"Ha! Jealous? Why would I be jealous? Who just had fantastic sex and two orgasms? Huh? Molly should be jealous of me."

He rolled and pinned her under him. "It's okay to be jealous."

"Great. You mean I have your permission? Thanks, pal!" she teased.

"Shut up, Sunshine, and kiss me."

Unable to turn down his generous offer, she did. And then she did some more kissing, and some other things, too, until they were both satisfied.

12

"Leave the Night On" by Sam Hunt

Shortly before midnight, D.C. left Sabrina, and snuck back into his room like a teenager who'd stayed out past his curfew. Funny, but it wasn't far from the truth since the B&B's lobby front doors were locked at midnight. He barely made it, thanks to the woman he couldn't get enough of. It would have been easier and less risky to stay the night.

But he never spent the night. It was Rule One. Spending the night gave a woman ideas. He wasn't going there, not when he'd already broken a rule with Sabrina. She had been more than worth breaking his perfect streak. Especially when she'd made it clear that she heard him. He wasn't going to fall in love.

Not with her and not with anyone.

Love turned people into damned fools who made decisions without first consulting their brains. Not going to happen. He'd locked his emotions up tight when living through what love for one man had done to his mother.

Back in his room, he pulled his clothes off again. Then he placed the western belt buckle in his briefcase for safe keeping. He'd never wear it. Still, he had a feeling he'd also never get rid of it. Sabrina made him laugh as much as she pissed him off. He'd rather remember the laughter. He took a quick shower, and as the warm water pounded on his back, he reviewed the evening.

He'd known Sabrina loved sex because she'd told him. Because she couldn't resist shoving that in his face at every turn. Oh, he believed her. Even before tonight, he'd believed her, but the reality had rocked him to the core. She was enthusiastic, passionate, and he wasn't lying when he said that she was addictive.

He would continue to tread carefully and never hurt her. All the usual parameters with a woman were in place. It wasn't like him to ever string anyone along, lie, and promise what he wouldn't deliver. Couldn't. For years, he'd had a plan. He was going to stick to that plan.

His mother had gone from a woman with occasional bouts of depression to slowly unraveling over the years. He'd grown up without a father. Later he'd learned that his biological father had never acknowledged her pregnancy, or him, and she clearly hadn't been strong enough to overcome that obstacle.

Her happiness had been tied up in being with one man she claimed to love. If that was love, he wanted no part of it. The way he saw it, love made a person weak. Had them making stupid choices and decisions they wouldn't otherwise. He'd left home on his scholarship, feeling guilt at being happy that he'd finally be free of the gloom and sadness of his mother's home.

Then guilt had crushed him when she'd been in a car accident shortly after he'd left home.

But now, now he would finally have peace. No more conflicts, when his entire adult life had been witnessing and then managing other people's conflicts. He'd have acres and acres of land. Horses. Time to ride and train them. Privacy.

Reminding himself he still had a job to do here, he pulled on a T-shirt and powered up his laptop, then went to the file he had on Sabrina Wilder. She wasn't going to be happy about the next step. He could already hear her complaints, but she'd do it.

Sooner or later she did everything asked of her, even if she was still reviewing whether performing was actually what she wanted to do with the rest of her life. She was still young. If she wanted to take some time off and go to school, or try something else for a change, she could do that. There would still be plenty of time for a comeback later. It wasn't an all or nothing proposition.

He went to the email correspondence between him and the reporter from *Country Music Scene*. Sabrina would face her first interview with the media post-scandal. She'd need to field the questions that would be lobbed in her direction and learn how to gracefully and tactfully answer them. For that, she'd first practice with him. He had a document with all the pre-submitted questions he'd allow the reporter to ask. Tomorrow morning, he'd find her and deal with this. Drill her all day if needed. Tomorrow night was up for grabs. He didn't see why there couldn't be an encore of tonight.

In fact, he was looking forward to it.

SABRINA WOKE up the next morning in a cold bed. Damien was gone, and so was his body heat. She had been prepared for that because he'd told her he wasn't going to stay. And there was no arguing that point. It made sense. She'd already slept with him once when she'd crawled in bed with him and woke the next morning spooning. Now she'd had mind-blowing sex with him. It might be nice to combine those two.

She was so worn out and sore that she wanted to call in sick. People did that, she knew, at jobs and such. She'd never had a real job though, and the only time she could ever take an unplanned day off had meant the flu accompanied by a high fever. Now she worked for herself in a way. The B&B belonged to her family. Her grandmother. How did one call in sick to their own grandmother? She couldn't do it. Anyway, Jessie would hunt her down. Then she'd see the afterglow on Sabrina's face and lay into her. But Sabrina hadn't made the same mistake twice. Damien wouldn't hurt her. He wouldn't use her.

But maybe she shouldn't have had sex with him. Okay, for sure she shouldn't have. First, she'd never been with a guy who made it clear that he *refused* to fall in love. She'd been the recipient of plenty of fan mail from men who said they were already in love with her when they didn't even know her. Offering marriage proposals. She supposed this thing with Damien was what people called casual sex, and she hadn't been raised that way. Mom would have a connip-tion fit if she knew, and her father would roll over in his grave. Twice. She deserved better than temporary. Her parents, hell, her sisters had drilled it into her.

A twinge of guilt shot down her spine because she would much rather have a real relationship. But she still didn't regret this. For all of his anti-love talk, Damien had been tender. Slow. They'd taken a shower together at some point, and he'd washed her hair. They'd wound up in bed again after the shower because she just couldn't resist him. He'd asked whether she was okay so many times she began to wonder if she looked sick. But no, he'd wanted to make sure she was enjoying him. She would have more of him, too, and as soon as possible.

She took a good look at her face in the bathroom mirror as she brushed her teeth and got ready for the day. Sex was definitely good for the complexion. Her skin was smooth and silky this morning with a little extra pink color. It had to be all the endorphins.

Loading up on coffee, she headed toward the B&B and the maid cart. Today she had to strip beds in two rooms and get them ready for the next guests. Rolling the cart into the Seaside room on the first floor, she plugged her earbuds in and went to her Spotify playlist. The first song was "Church" by Maren Morris. One of her favorites, and a song she wished she could have recorded. She would love to have the talent to write a song like that. It said everything she believed about music. Often, country music felt like her church. It felt like her salvation.

Her religion.

She sang along as she stripped the first bed. The maid job gave her time to listen to music and not feel guilty about it. She could also think without distractions. Because she had to figure out what *she* wanted to do with the rest of her life. Not what Lexi wanted, or what her mother wanted. Both wanted her back in Nashville. Sabrina had thought she wanted that, too, and never considered any other possibility until Damien gave her permission to decide for herself.

Until that moment, she hadn't realized that she had a choice. Her entire life from the time she was ten had been mapped out for her. She'd loved her former life, but what if there was something else? Something better. And why had no one other than Damien ever asked her what *she* wanted?

She decided right then and there that she would do some research of her own. She had a little time while she waited to see if there was any interest from Nashville. She could find out what other jobs she might like. Make-up artist would be fun, and she'd already learned so much over the years. She'd have an in with celebrities in Nashville. Heck, her own sister.

Or she could learn how to design clothes! Her own fashion label, maybe. She'd always been such a fan of fashion. And shoes. Then, of course, there were all the lost causes that needed her help. Ever since she'd seen the first commercial about abandoned pets on TV, she'd been giving regularly. What if she started a business to save injured dogs and cats?

Sabrina tucked the edge of one sheet in its corner and then reached across the bed to tuck the other one in. She went around to the end of the bed and tucked a third corner in. As usual, it didn't want to stretch so she pulled on it as hard as she could. For the last corner, there was not enough room. She didn't understand why sheets were never big enough for the beds.

There should be a better design. The sheet didn't look right once the fourth corner was somewhat tucked in. She might have the sheet reversed. Pulling it off, she tried again. Tugging at the last corner with all her might, she heard the loud sound of a rip.

She groaned. "Oh, no. Not again."

Gran was going to kill her. Sabrina threw the difficult sheet into the cart and grabbed another one. On her playlist, Miranda Lambert had just declared how her gun was bigger than a man's fist, and Sabrina really thought she might get the sheet to cooperate this time, when someone grabbed her from behind.

She nearly had a heart attack, and then had a small one when she turned to see Kit Wilder. Mom. Last month, she'd visited for a short while, but before that she'd stayed away so long that Sabrina had become used to life without her.

"Geez, you scared me." She pulled her earbuds out.

"I've got good news." Mom held her arms out. "I sold the condo, and I'm moving back to Whistle Cove!"

"That's...great." Though Jessie might not like it much. She pretty much ran things around here, and she and Mom butted heads often.

"I'm taking Lexi's old service cottage."

"Does Gran know?"

Things had just started to calm down. No one in Whistle Cove talked about her *indiscretion* anymore. It was behind them, and they understood Sabrina had made a mistake, and she was forgiven. But Mom had a way of bringing the drama with her. She was a dead ringer for Samantha from *Sex and the City*, with all the great clothes and style. But without all the promiscuity.

"Do you really think she'd turn away her only daughter-in-law? The mother of her granddaughters?"

"No, but she'd probably like to know what's going on."

"I'll tell her right after I find Jessie." Kit glanced at the unmade bed and frowned. "Honey, you've got the sheet on sideways."

"I do? I thought it was sideways the first time."

Mom went around the other side of the bed. She switched the sheet's direction, snapped it so that it laid out all on its own, then went around tucking corners and smoothing it over like some kind of a professional.

"I haven't figured this out yet," Sabrina said. But she would. Surely a sheet couldn't best her.

"That's because you don't have any business making other people's beds. People should be making the bed for you." Mom finished by smoothing the tight center down one last time.

Sabrina didn't appreciate it when Mom made her sound like someone who couldn't be bothered with menial chores. Like a diva. "I don't mind helping. Gran needs me. Especially with Lexi gone."

"You've been such a big help. But I'm here now, and I'll take over. You should just concentrate on getting back to Nashville. I know Lexi misses you."

"Sure," Sabrina said, unwilling to share her possible new direction with Mom. She'd strike it down like enemy fire.

Mom had been hopeful that all of her daughters would get back to the music business sooner rather than later. She would have helped if she had the connections that her father had, but she didn't. Still, she and Daddy had been both of a mindset that Sabrina was born to perform. Maybe they were right, but how would she know there was nothing else she'd rather do if she didn't at least consider the idea?

"I'm going to go find Jessie and get the key. I've got a couple of suitcases with me, but the rest of my things are being shipped."

"Tony will help you with the luggage," Sabrina said.

"And I should also meet this fixer man that Luke sent for you. How's that going?" She quickly appraised Lexi's outfit, the simple working uniform of the B&B: jeans and a long-sleeved branded polo shirt. "I'm glad to see you're back to dressing normally and not in one of your ridiculous costumes."

Mom loved fashion as much as Sabrina did and had

both sewn and chosen all of her earlier wardrobe for years. Now, Sabrina pictured Mom meeting Damien. Then a huge freeway pile-up after an accident. It was the first image that came to mind. This wouldn't be good. Both had strong personalities, and if Damien had thought *she* was difficult, wait until he met her mother.

"Damien's great. I went to Hollywood a few days ago and...met a few industry professionals." *And had a meltdown, but let's not go there.*

"How exciting!"

"Yeah, it was nice. I'm learning so much from him about image and handling fame and the press."

"Damien Caldwell, right?"

"He likes everyone to call him D.C. And I got a new wardrobe." Sabrina got excited. Few people in her inner circle would appreciate her new clothes like Mom would. "Wait till you see this dress!"

"Is it very shiny?"

Sabrina was about to tell her mom that the dress might be seen from space it was so glittery, but Jessie appeared in the doorway. "Mom?"

"Sweetheart! Surprise!" Mom flew into Jessie's arms. "I'm home to stay."

"Since when?" From over Mom's shoulder, Jessie made a face and mouthed: *did you know about this*?

Sabrina shrugged and mouthed back: *No idea.*

"Since you all need my help around here." Kit pulled back, her neck swiveling duck-like. "And I can take Lexi's old cottage."

"Well," Jessie said. "I was going to offer the room to Olga in case she ever needed to stay overnight."

"Don't be silly. She wouldn't want to be away from Tony even for a single night. I know because I was the same way with your blessed father." She sniffed, waving her hand as if to tamp down the tears. "Oh, my. Don't get me started."

"Aw, Mom." Sabrina came to hug her from behind, and then all three of them were in a group hug.

"Remember when your daddy would have all five of us hug it out before each performance? You girls were so little. Where did the time go?" She squeezed tighter.

"I'm sorry," Jessie said. "I didn't mean to sound ungrateful. We can always use the extra help around here."

"Yeah," Sabrina said. "So much to do running a B&B. I never had any idea."

Mom waved a hand dismissively. "It's housework, and I've done my share of that."

Jessie turned to Sabrina. "I actually came looking for you for a reason. D.C. wants to talk to you."

"Okay, but I'm not done with this room. I just had a little trouble with the sheets."

"Again?" Jessie went hand on hip.

"You try making these beds! I still say the sheets are the wrong size."

"For the last time, they're *not* the wrong size. How many times do I have to tell you—"

"Now, now, girls. Please. Let's calm down," Mom said. "Sabrina, you go ahead and check in with D.C. I'm sure he's got more important things for you to do. I'll take care of the rooms."

Both Sabrina and Jessie turned to Mom, jaws gaping.

Mom couldn't be serious. She wore black high-heeled pumps and a matching pencil skirt paired with a silk blouse. She glanced down at her outfit and laughed.

"Well, quick, somebody get me a uniform!"

13

"You Make it Easy" by Jason Aldean

Sabrina headed to the deck where Jessie had informed her Damien waited. If he wanted an answer on what she'd decided about her future, she didn't even want to tell him she was contemplating anything other than Nashville. If she didn't choose Nashville, he'd have no incentive to stick around. Even if she understood she had no future with him, Sabrina wasn't ready to say goodbye.

But she'd get there. Her old life had meant saying goodbye every few months to new friends. When she got back from the road, everyone had moved on. There were new cliques and alliances. She didn't fit in with anyone but her sisters. After a while, she'd stopped trying.

This should be no different, then, except that this time he'd be the one to leave. Granted, she wasn't used to that. But he had to get back to his precious cattle ranch. Eventually, she imagined, he'd find a woman who was a better match for him. Someone who wanted to live home on the range.

She wondered if that woman would have to slaughter cows or milk them. It might almost be possible to feel sorry for her. But at the moment, she wanted to wrap her hands around the neck of this imaginary woman and squeeze. *Sabrina* wanted him. He was hers, and she was his. He'd said so. For now.

She found him at a table, hunched over his laptop. The wind kicked up, and blew his dark locks around, giving him a Heathcliff from *Wuthering Heights* look. He glanced up as she approached, and the hint of a smile tipped his lips. His eyes were soft and warm. Her heart gave a powerful tug.

"Sit," he ordered and pointed to the chair across from his own.

"Um, you need to ask nicely."

His brows scrunched together, and a tiny flash of scary calm crossed in his gaze.

"Because, you know, our relationship is a little different now. You should ask and not order."

His eyes darkened. "Why not? You seemed to like my orders last night."

"That's...different." Her face flushed.

"You're not going to sit until I *ask* you to sit?"

"I'll sit down when I feel like it if you don't ask nicely."

He shrugged and went back to his laptop. "Suit yourself."

It shouldn't have surprised her that he wouldn't even budge on this tiny thing. He was such an infuriating alpha man! After three minutes of standing, she took a seat. Not across from him. Next to him. Then she laid a hand on his thigh. He quirked a brow.

"What? I decided I wanted to sit down."

"That's not what I meant." He glanced down at her hand. "No one can see us."

He nodded. "Tell me, baby. Why do you have to fight me on every little thing?"

"Because it's fun."

He took her hand but rather than move it, he set it further up his thigh. "Ought not to make it fun anymore. I should take you over my lap and give you a spanking."

"Huh. Well, I'm not really into that, but I read the book."

He snorted and didn't respond to that. "Back to work. I have an interview scheduled for you with a representative from *Country Music Scene.* Day after tomorrow. You need to be ready for it. There may be some hard-hitting questions."

She hadn't expected that this soon in the process. Her experience with the media hadn't been at all positive in more than a year. They'd hounded her for interviews. Her story. They all wanted an explanation. An exclusive. Rather than give them what they wanted, she and her sisters had retreated to Whistle Cove where the residents mostly left them alone.

"Okay. I'll talk about anything except the photo."

"That's *exactly* what you're going to talk about. Your fans want to hear from you. Not from the loser who sold the photo, not the tabloid who published it, and not the recording label. You."

"But—"

"No room for negotiation on this one. Frankly, you should have gotten ahead of this story the moment you heard about it. If you get in front of a scandal, admit what you've done wrong, and apologize, there's nothing left to gossip about anymore. No more rumor and innuendo. Just the facts. Takes the wind right out of their freaking sails."

She took her hand back, ready to fight. "I don't like

talking about it. It's so humiliating. Makes me look like an idiot. Which I was."

He met her eyes. "You may not like talking about it, but you will."

She squirmed, hearing the no-nonsense tone in his voice. "What do I say?"

"I'm going to walk you through it, but we can start with how you explained it to me. Just that simple."

"O-okay. How many people read this blog?"

"Their circulation is close to a million."

"A *million*?"

She doubted that many people would be interested in her sad story, but then she remembered how many people on the freeway were fascinated by a car accident. Everyone had to slow down enough to see all the damage. It was hard to look away from that kind of thing. A million people would be reading about the biggest mistake of her life, when up until that lousy day, she'd been such a good girl. She still considered herself to be a good girl. She loved her grandma, mom, and sisters. She'd never hurt a single soul on purpose. Once, at the height of her fame, her parents had discussed how she could be an example to young girls everywhere.

Guess now she'd be a cautionary tale.

"Fine! But that TV doctor is where I draw the line." She swished an imaginary line in the air. "You see that? That right there is the line."

He smirked. "You got it. No TV doctors."

Since he'd hit her with some not-so-pleasant news, she figured he deserved fair warning of a cold front coming in. Her mother might want a part in all this. She'd want to look at the questions and give her input, too.

"My mom showed up today. She's moving back which is

a little bit of a surprise. I didn't know she'd be coming, but for a while she's talked about moving back home. Now she's here for good."

"You can introduce me later."

She nodded. "You know, my parents got me into this business, and now that it's just my mother...let's just say she's invested."

"Understood."

"Okay, but you've been warned. She might want to look at the questions ahead of time."

"She won't get what she wants."

Oh boy.

ALMOST TWO HOURS LATER, D.C. had drilled Sabrina on all the questions. The ones he'd pre-approved with the journalist and which accomplished their purpose. He was surprised to see her only argue with him ten more times before she gave in. Always happened. Eventually. She just wasn't easy. In fact, she'd made this job a lot more difficult than it would have been with anyone else. But given these same circumstances, by now he'd have long left this job in his rear-view if it had been anybody but her.

While he would share that information with her, he worried that she might make more out of it than she should. He'd already spent the night with her before they'd had sex, even if it was completely unintentional. She'd been at her rock bottom in the bathroom of that hotel room, and an intimacy had grown between them that went far beyond the physical.

It completely unnerved him.

There was also the fact that she saw right through him

when no one else ever had. He'd gotten used to being alone, and he didn't like the idea of changing now, but she of all people *saw* him.

"One last time," he said. "Statement."

She did her eye roll thing. "I'm so sorry if I hurt any of my loyal fans, but I made a terrible mistake. I trusted someone I shouldn't have. I did something impulsive that is not part of my real character. This was my mistake, and I don't blame anyone else. I've moved beyond that part of my life and hope that others will be able to forgive me like I've finally forgiven myself."

"Good." Each time the statement was a little different, but he liked that better than a canned response. Sounded far more believable.

"Can we take a break now?" She stretched her arms in the air.

He was sufficiently satisfied that she would sail through the interview as long as she followed his directions. Orders, as she would say. Either way.

"Sure, you probably need to get back to work." And he should make a call about the offer on the ranch.

He shut his laptop and stood. She was still sitting and looking up at him expectantly. "You don't want me to ask you to stand, do you?"

"Ha, ha. No, I...I just wanted to ask you to come over later." She avoided his eyes. "Tonight."

"What? No snappy sexual innuendo? *Now* you're being shy with me?"

When she met his gaze, it was strangely vulnerable. "I got nothing."

He tugged her up. "That's because you don't need to joke about it anymore. *It* happened."

"Yeah, I just hope *it* will happen again. Tonight. Three times because good things come in threes."

"*There* she is."

She smiled at him. Soft eyes shimmering, both hands skimmed up his forearms to his biceps. That simple touch from her had him on fire, thinking on whether it would be possible to sneak in an afternoon session. No reason to wait until the sun went down. No reason, that is, other than the fact that he shouldn't blatantly advertise this thing between them.

It wasn't his career that concerned him any longer or his reputation. He worried about her. Although he wasn't noble enough to stay away, he still had to protect her. Image could be everything. All the media had to do was catch wind that she'd taken up with the very man come to *repair* her image, and maybe all their hard work would be undone.

That meant the cover of darkness.

"Name the time," he said, reminding himself he was thirty-two and not seventeen again.

Leaving Sabrina until later, he walked to his room, deposited his laptop, and changed for a run. Then he phoned Annie King to get an update on his offer. She hadn't called back, which had him curious.

"Hi, D.C.," she said. "I was going to call you."

"What's the latest?"

"It's not good," she began. "They got another offer in. The new buyer is offering twice the asking price."

D.C. cursed. "*Twice?*"

This didn't make sense. Why would anyone pay twice the market value price? Unless...

"It's exactly what you're thinking. He got wind you were trying to buy it."

It was like all the oxygen had been knocked out of him. He should have known this would happen. His damned egotistical sperm donor couldn't stand for D.C. to own a cattle ranch. Too close to his birthright, he imagined. Besides, his father's family might eventually put it together when another Caldwell, one they didn't know, owned substantial land.

Damien had toyed with the idea of naming it the Caldwell Ranch just to piss the man off. He'd keep to his end of the bargain and never ask for his inheritance, but if someone else came along and figured it out, he couldn't do much about that, could he?

He cursed a blue streak. "Have the Farrells accepted yet?"

"Surprisingly, no."

He spoke through gritted teeth. "You're serious."

"I am. But I'm worried. How long can someone hold out on an offer like that?"

"Why the hell didn't you call me right away?"

She hesitated. "I've been thinking about how I could break this to you."

He cursed again. "Never delay again. Never. I'll match the fucking offer."

There was silence on the other end for a moment. "But matching this offer...don't you want to consult with your broker first? This is—"

"Don't need to consult with anyone. Make. The. Offer. And *never* hold out on me again." D.C. hung up, fury consuming him. It sat in his gut like fire.

He didn't want them to accept his offer simply because they might hate to see it go to the senior Caldwell, who was buying up ranches as fast as he could get his hand on them. D.C. wanted to beat the old man fair and square. He paced the room, thinking of the jackass who believed he could beat him.

The man who didn't have the balls to recognize his own son. Image. Yeah, it mattered. It mattered to the man who had portrayed himself as a family man to the core and yet had impregnated a much younger woman. D.C.'s mother. That man had a carefully crafted image that didn't have much to do with reality.

He'd destroyed D.C.'s mother bit by bit. She'd gone from the vibrant, beautiful woman who'd once been a Miss Texas to the "other woman" cast aside. Rather than fight back, she'd retreated, hurt and damaged. Weak from her intense love for a man who wanted nothing more to do with her. That kind of overwhelming love and addiction to someone destroyed from the inside out. He'd been the dutiful son and taken care of his mother for years, enduring her bouts of depression, and doing what he could.

His plans had been to take care of her even better if he'd managed the long shot to the NFL. Buy her a beautiful home. Hire a full-time caretaker in case she ever tried to hurt herself, as he'd secretly always feared she would. When he'd lost his scholarship, it was more than his own future on the line. She'd died in a car accident a year after he'd gone to university, releasing D.C. from his promise that he'd never ask his biological father for a dime.

But his father had no idea who he was dealing with any longer. He only knew the man who'd accepted a settlement for agreeing to never disclose he was his illegitimate son. He remembered *that* kid, desperate and in trouble with nowhere else to turn. He'd taken what he could get and parlayed his small payday into something much larger.

D.C. had the money to match his father's offer. It made no

sense to pay more than the place was worth, but the pleasure he'd feel at ripping it from his deadbeat father's grasp would more than make up for it. After ten minutes of pacing in his room, he realized he had an entire beach at his disposal and set off for a run. He passed other joggers, some of them with their dogs, going at a much slower pace. Left them in the dust.

He ran until he could hear the loud thud of his heartbeat in his ears. When his temper had cooled enough, he turned back, slowing down and coaxing his body to do the same. Sweat beads slithered down his back and face. He wiped them away with the back of his hand. He needed a shower.

He needed Sabrina. Tonight, he would bury himself inside her. He'd tell her all the dirty things he was about to do to her. No more holding back. She wasn't a kid at all, but a woman who'd been facing some of the shit he'd faced at a much younger age. But there was one marked difference. She'd always had her family, and they'd had her back.

D.C. hadn't had anyone since his mother passed away. No brothers or sisters, at least none who knew about him or would ever recognize him as one of the Dallas Caldwells. But he'd had a mentor who'd been like a father, and he had a handful of true friends he could count on for anything. The type who'd help him bury a body, if needed, and ask no questions.

Later D.C. spent some time speaking with the journalist who would interview Sabrina. Felicia Tyler was excited, as she should be. This interview was a bit of a coup, and she was a young reporter D.C. had thrown a bone. She'd once done him a favor and pulled a negative story on one of his clients simply because he'd asked.

He knew it went a little further than a simple favor out of kindness. She'd had a crush on him, and he'd used that to his favor. He'd guaranteed that he'd repay her someday, and that day had come. The questions were all pre-approved by D.C., but there were no softballs, either.

He took care of a few more phone calls and emails, and finally made the phone call he'd been avoiding. It was time.

"Hey, dude," Luke answered.

D.C. had his private cell number, as he did with all of his clients. He could be trusted never to give it out, and everyone knew it. "Checking in."

"How's Operation Wildest Sister going?"

"You weren't lying. She's a handful."

"Yeah, well, I warned you." He chuckled. "But she's on board with what you're trying to do?"

"We've made some progress." And now to the issue he wanted to bring up. "After you hired me, I used some of my contacts at Rise Up. Made some connections. The Los Angeles branch was more than interested, but that's not going to work out."

"L.A.?"

"Surprised?"

"Well, yeah. Sabrina's practically a Nashville fixture. Or she was."

"Those seem to be her feelings as well." Neglecting to mention the meltdown, knowing now that she was as strong as he wanted her to be, D.C. went on to explain his progress and his plans. "I've got interest from the biggest label in Nashville."

"That's...amazing." He spoke off line, presumably to Lexi.

"There's something you should know," D.C. said, prepared for some pushback. "I've asked Sabrina to decide for herself if this come-back is what she really wants."

There was silence on the other end, and then Luke finally spoke. "And?"

"Seemed like no one had ever asked her that before."

"Know what? That's probably true. She was almost born into this business."

"I think she should decide for herself."

"You're right."

"She's still thinking it over. In the meantime, we keep moving forward."

"Man, you do have a set of balls on you. Gotta believe Kit didn't take that well."

"No idea. She doesn't know."

Luke exhaled. "She will. And you're going to hear about it. Kit has definite ideas on her daughters' careers. She and John Wilder crafted the original image they had. A wholesome family with well-behaved daughters."

"That image has left the building. Her daughters are grown women with minds of their own. Especially the youngest."

"You don't have to tell me that. But you might have to tell Kit." Luke laughed.

"No one tells me how to do my job."

"Knew I liked you."

D.C. hung up, satisfied, but found himself unable to drop the pissy mood. Running had cooled him down from his previous semi-homicidal mood, but the same rage still sat in his gut, directed toward the senior Caldwell. The man was costing D.C. more money. Money he'd worked hard for years to accumulate. Sure, he could find another ranch, but he wasn't going to back down now. Not for a minute. Not when he could match the old man's offer.

D.C. almost wished he could be in the same room when the fucker heard the news that his offer had been matched.

It would mean he'd either have to walk away from the deal or throw more money at it. He wouldn't want to throw more money at it when he'd already doubled the asking price, mistakenly thinking that he'd close the deal instantly. Mistakenly thinking that D.C. was the same scared kid who'd taken his conditional help.

Pretty soon, he realized nothing else was going to help but seeing Sabrina, so he headed out to grab dinner at a local seafood place on the wharf. Along the boardwalk, he found his pick of vendors. Stores lined the wharf, selling touristy items and plenty of food from fish to saltwater taffy. There were high quality restaurants as well as vendors selling everything from shrimp cocktails to fried fish. He showed up at Sabrina's cottage loaded down with clam chowder bread bowls, fried calamari, and fries.

"Ooooh!" Sabrina said when she opened the door to him.

"You hungry?"

"Sure! Wow. I didn't think you'd bring me dinner." She sashayed into the kitchen, and he followed that tantalizing ass, something close to mesmerized.

"Why not? You think this is just a booty call?"

Sabrina simply turned back to flash a smile at him. "You make that sound like a bad thing."

He set the package of food on the table in her small kitchen. Never having been in the kitchen which was at the back of the cottage, he noticed that Sabrina kept it neat and tidy in here. Either that or she never cooked. A distinct possibility he didn't discount. The dark wood table was small with only two stools.

Sabrina helped unpack the food, then went through her cupboards looking for plates, spoons, and forks, which she set on the table. They both dug in, going for the bread bowls first. The New England clam chowder from the Monterey Wharf was first rate, D.C. had found, and in some cases, even award-winning. Well-deserved, too.

Sabrina broke off a piece of bread and dunked it in the chowder. "This is my favorite meal. I could live on bread. Don't tell anyone, but I think I might have been a carb in another life."

He chuckled, the first one of the day, as it turned out, but then quickly became entranced by the way she ate. Lusty and sensual. Like the way she sang.

"What?" she said, licking her lips after a dribble of soup had escaped. "Do I have something on my face?"

"Not anymore." If it happened again, *he* would lick it off. "Got some news today, and I'm going to have to cut this short. Need to get back to Texas. There's a bit of a problem with the ranch I want."

"Oh." She wouldn't meet his eyes as she dipped the spoon back in the bread bowl. "Your ranch?"

"Yeah. If I don't get back soon, I'll *have* no ranch."

"What do you mean?"

"Someone else made an offer, double the asking price. I had to match it."

"Why would someone offer double the price?"

Why indeed. "To close the deal."

"I don't know much about ranches, but isn't there another one around you could buy?"

"Sure. I want this one."

"You always get what you want, don't you?"

That was almost funny. "Not even close, Sunshine."

She stopped eating then, and he wished he hadn't brought this up until later. "What about me?"

"My work here is done. The interview tomorrow will conclude our business. She's a reporter who owes me a favor, and she's going to ask you only pre-submitted questions. You'll be portrayed in a favorable light. She's got the scoop, and that's huge for her. Now you've got interest from several labels, and it's just a matter of you flying out to Nashville to look over contracts and sign with one of them. Frankly, I've overstepped my bounds here. Your agent or manager should take care of the rest from here."

"I guess my manager will be my mother."

"Kit Wilder?" *That* was disturbing.

He'd rather have her with someone who had experience in the more recent world of the Nashville music business scene. If she wasn't careful, she'd sign all her rights away. Her future. But Lexi Wilder wouldn't allow that to happen. Luke would also have some input. They could guide her the rest of the way.

"It used to be my father. She's going to want to do it now. The only reason she's not doing that for Lexi is because she went with Luke's management. It just made sense." She shrugged.

"You can consider them, too, or I can make some referrals. Family and business don't always make the best combination. You need a powerhouse behind you."

"Okay," she said, looking disheartened. She was very attached to her family. That was clear to anyone with half a brain. "I'll think about it."

A cloud had come over her gaze.

"What's wrong, baby?"

"You're leaving. This is our last night. Then the interview tomorrow, and you're off to be a cowboy. Right?"

"Right. But you knew that—"

"I know, I know. I know you're leaving. You don't fall in love. You don't do relationships. But I'm going to miss you anyway if that's okay with you."

Not at all. It wasn't okay with him. At least, the pinch in his chest at hearing she'd miss him was very much *not* okay. He didn't want her to miss him any more than he wanted to miss her. He wanted her to go on without him and leave him in the dust. Alone at last. But when she climbed off her stool and joined him on his, straddling him, he lost words. They were right there on the tip of his tongue. *It's not okay. Move on. Don't count on me for anything.* He just couldn't say them out loud when she kissed his neck.

"Who tried to take the ranch from you?"

Yeah. It was hard to focus when she did that thing with her tongue. "Just a nearby rancher who has too much but can never get enough."

"Who is he? You know him, right?"

He stiffened when her hands went under his shirt. Because of the question and because of the warm fingers splayed across his abs. "How do you know?"

"You said to listen to what people are not telling you as much as what they're telling you. And you know that man, whoever he is. You know him, and you hate him. I want to know why."

She was a quick study, this one. How could this girl, he meant *woman*, six years younger than him, read him so well? Either he wasn't the soulless man he thought he was, or she had some kind of insight into his mind that no one else had.

"How do you *know* I hate him?" His hands tightened around her waist as she gyrated into his erection.

"It's in the way your jaw gets tight when you mention him. Is he your mortal enemy?"

He couldn't help but chuckle. "Close. And if we're going to do this, we'll do it my way."

14

"Cry Pretty" by Carrie Underwood

abrina was firmly removed from Damien's lap just when she was getting into her erotic lap dance. Undulating her hips as best as she could, she'd felt his hard promise for tonight. And she was going to do her best to wear him out. Their last night, and she would make it count. She stayed planted on the floor in front of him, curious as to what he meant by "his way" when as far as she could tell, his body was enjoying "her way."

"Take off your clothes," he ordered.

"Now? *Here*?"

She looked down at her outfit. A pair of purple wooly socks, blue jeans, and a white fisherman's sweater. She'd never taken off her clothes in the kitchen. Everyone knew that being naked in the kitchen was dangerous, and not just because of the way her heart was currently racing at stroke levels. His eyes had darkened to almost black with their blazing heat.

"Yeah. For each question you ask, and I answer, you take something off."

"Deal." She removed one wooly sock and smiled at his scowl. "Who is he?"

"My father."

"Your *father*?"

"Yes," he answered quickly. "Take something else off."

"No fair. That one wasn't really a question. You already answered it." At his quirked eyebrow, she took the other sock off, sighing heavily. "You're cheating."

He leaned against the counter, arms crossed. "Hey, you're the one with all of the questions."

"Why do you hate him?" She removed her sweater, revealing her black lacy bra.

With a wolfish grin, he answered, "He makes it easy."

"That's not an answer!"

He lifted a shoulder. She went hands on hips and cocked her head until he gave in.

"Short answer? I didn't grow up with him. He refuses to acknowledge I'm his son."

Her heart fell to her toes while she considered her next question. This time she shimmied out of her jeans and cast them to the side. "Why?"

Damien's eyes took her in, his gaze sweeping from her exposed stomach to her legs. "Nice."

"You didn't answer the question!"

He went palms up. "He was already married when he got my mother pregnant. And getting the waitress at his favorite golf resort pregnant was not fitting with the image of a devout family man. He's filthy rich and has a way of buying people off for their silence."

Sabrina sucked in a breath, outraged for him. "He bought your silence, too?"

He took a step toward her and stared until she unsnapped her bra and removed it.

"Remember the trouble I got into when I lost my scholarship?" At her nod, he continued. "It was the first and last time I went to him. My mother had refused to ask him for anything when he didn't leave his wife for her. I needed help getting through college once the scholarship money was gone. I figured the man owed my mother even if he owed me nothing. He introduced me to the man who made his problems go away, paid for my college tuition, and asked me never to contact him again. He had me sign an agreement that I'd never ask for a DNA test or speak to the press about our relationship. It was only then that I realized for certain I was his son. And he knew it, too."

Heart aching for him, she slipped out of her panties. Naked and completely exposed to him, she asked her last question, because she had to know. "Where's your mom now?"

"She'd always struggled." The tone of his voice was flat. Removed. "She died in a car accident years ago."

Her heart shattered then, just broke into a thousand pieces, and she stayed rooted to her spot on the cold kitchen tile floor. She was vaguely aware she was shivering now, naked, and bare to him.

"Baby, I'm so sorry." She went into his arms and plastered her body against his. "I wish I'd known that."

"You're strong, Sunshine, stronger than she ever was. She let the world beat her down. Maybe it was because of my father, maybe it was just who she was. I don't know. But once someone knocked her down, she never got up again." Hand on the nape of her neck, he gripped her tightly, making a point.

She understood. Sabrina had gotten up again. But she'd

say that was not just because she'd been taught how to be strong, but because she had two equally tough sisters who always had her back. A family who'd stayed strong for the small amount of time when she couldn't be. But Damien's mother might not have had that kind of support. The someone who'd knocked her down was the man Damien hated. For good reason. She didn't want him to go to Texas, but she also needed him to have his ranch, if only to take it away from that horrible man.

Her eyes watery, she fought to control her emotions but her lower lip trembled. "You're going to get that ranch and be a bigger and better cowboy than he ever was."

"Rancher," he said, hands on her behind as he hauled her into his arms. "I will be, but not tonight. Tonight is about us."

He carried her from the kitchen into the bedroom, laying her down on the bed like precious cargo. For someone who was so bossy and domineering, he could be unbelievably gentle at times. And she loved the way he made her feel. Loved it when he hungrily took in her imperfect body, which didn't seem to matter to him. His, on the other hand, was molded like steel.

But he obviously worked at it and probably didn't have the same addiction to chocolate and potato chips that she did. Even though tonight wasn't their first time, it still felt that way to her. Eyes riveted on him, she watched as he kicked off his boots and slowly unbuttoned his shirt, not once breaking eye contact. He threw his shirt aside and went for his pants.

"Wait. Let me. Please." She kneeled on the edge of the bed and stayed his hands.

He let her take over and she unbuttoned and unzipped his pants. Then her fingers slowly drifted down his abs and back up to his pecs. She followed with her tongue, licking her way down to the waistband of his pants. Then she pulled on his pants and underwear until she could reach inside and take him in her hands. Enjoying the hiss that tore out of him, she stroked him over and over again. He tensed in her hand to the consistency of marble.

"Enough," he said and tackled her to the bed. "My turn."

"You're very bossy, you know?"

"I know, and you love it."

"Sometimes."

There was something to be said for a man who ordered her to let go of every last one of her inhibitions. Who ordered her to enjoy every wonderful and wicked thing he was doing to her body. They were skin to skin, belly to belly, sliding against each other in a tangle of arms, legs, and hips. He sought her lips and kissed her, his tongue warm and wet and insistent. Demanding. She opened to him, her bones melting, and she grew weak under his ministrations. There was just no other word for it. He had her. He'd had her from day one.

His mouth lowered to the column of her neck, his tongue leaving a hot branding path as he made his way south. He sucked in a nipple, teasing her with his tongue until the nipple was one hard peak. He gave equal attention to both breasts, slowly whipping her into a frenzy of hot pulsating desire. She'd never known anything like this all-consuming need that ripped through her body. She was desperate to have him inside her, tugged on his buttock, and tried to make it happen.

He wasn't cooperating.

"Look at me," he suddenly growled, and she realized only then her eyes were closed against the intensity of her sweet agony. "I want you to see who's doing this to you.

Who's going to make you come harder than you ever have."

"I'm looking at you," she said, eyes locked on his gaze.

He didn't break eye contact and the moment was both erotic and intimate. She felt linked to him in a bigger way than she'd ever expected or planned. A mixture of both pleasure and fear now rocked through her as he continued his slow torture.

"Please. Now." She tugged on him. "Get in me."

"Love when you beg," he said as he crawled back up her body.

Moments later he'd ripped a condom packet open with his teeth and protected them both. He rolled her, so she was on top, and then lifted her on him as if she weighed nothing.

"Damn, I like this view," he said on a ragged breath.

His gaze ate her up, but his hands were on her hips, moving her on him in a steady rhythm. He was deep inside her, going deeper each time, then moving her off him only to do it again and again. The delicious pressure and friction rose inside her, and she gripped his shoulders to have something to cling to as her world spun out of control.

"Baby," she moaned and cried out as her body tensed and convulsed. Waves of pleasure hit her hard, one after another.

He joined her a moment later, and at the sound of his guttural groan her pleasure mixed with his in an irresistible combination.

This was it, she realized as they slowed together, coming down from the peak.

He'd ruined her for all other men.

~

IT WASN'T until hours later, when he was still lying in bed, his arms full of Sabrina, that D.C. wondered why he'd told her about his mother. He didn't discuss that part of his life with anyone, not even those closest to him. It was both painful and humiliating. For a long time, he'd been angry and ashamed that she'd been so weak. Then he'd met real desperation and been forced to reach out to his father.

Only then had he understood how someone could feel so small and insignificant that it took too much energy and strength to bounce back. He wasn't one of those people. He got up again, fists swinging. And so had Sabrina. Realizing he had nothing to do with it, he was still proud of her.

Even when she'd pissed him off. She was a fighter, like him. And she was currently singing to him.

"Have you thought any more on what we talked about?"

"Yes, I *know*. You're leaving. It's okay."

He tried to ignore the small flash of irritation he felt that she'd taken his leaving sooner so easily. "Not that. Talking about whether you've decided music is what you want to do for the rest of your life."

"I'm still thinking."

"Think fast, because you're going to get an offer soon. Don't feel pressure to say yes right away. It will give you a little more time."

"Do you do this with all your clients?" She went up on one elbow. "Do you ask them if they're doing what they want to do with their life?"

"No, but I probably should have. You're also the first client I've had that didn't ever have a real choice."

"It isn't like I *hated* what I was doing. I really loved singing and performing with my sisters, and my parents knew it."

"It will be different now, on your own."

"I know." She sighed. "And that's scary. It just can't be the reason I decide."

"Damn straight." This woman. She was tough inside but soft on the outside.

He couldn't deny he would miss her sass and spunk. Yeah, okay, he would miss a whole hell of a lot more. Too damn bad her life was the very opposite of what he wanted for the next stage of his. Because he had no doubt she'd choose music. It wasn't just what she did but *who* she was. She'd soon come to that realization, if she hadn't already.

She couldn't stop singing, and it would be a damn shame for the music world if she did. She'd have a very public life. He'd been through enough conflict and looked forward to a peaceful life. A life when he'd travel only where and when he wanted.

"Can you spend the night with me? Sleep with me."

"I better not, Sunshine."

She sat up straight. "Why? Because of some stupid rule you have?"

"Yeah." A one-word answer. He was having a difficult time ignoring her rosy pink nipples, and his gaze slipped to her naked breasts.

She pulled the sheet up to cover herself, forcing him to meet her eyes. "That's what I thought. It's a stupid rule. You don't need to worry about me wanting a marriage proposal or anything. You've leaving tomorrow, so what's the big deal? Are you afraid I'm going to stalk you? Follow you out to your cattle ranch?"

"I'm not afraid of that."

"I don't even *like* cows!"

He quirked a brow at this because, seriously, how could anyone not like cows? "What about horses?"

"I like horses. They're beautiful." She climbed out of bed

and reached for a robe then pointed at him. "And you're trying to change the subject."

"Where are you going?"

"Popcorn." She shuffled to the kitchen and he followed her, pulling on his underwear.

She may have been buck naked in the kitchen for him, but he didn't feel like being quite that physically vulnerable. If there were going to be any cooked nuts in here, they sure wouldn't be his.

"Are we having our first fight?" he asked.

"First? Ha!" She riffled through her cabinets, coming up with a sealed bag of microwave popcorn. "Obviously, you can't count."

"I meant first fight as lovers."

"First and last, I guess. It's not like we had much time." She set the bag in the microwave and furiously punched buttons.

"You're pissed because I don't want to spend the night."

"Bingo! Give the man a prize."

"Great. Can my prize be that you come back to bed and take some of that anger out on me in there?" He grinned, hoping to ease the tension of the moment.

She scoffed. "I'm mad because you have such little faith in me."

"Not true."

"If you believed me, then you wouldn't be so stubborn."

"Baby, next time you think 'stubborn' go look in a mirror."

"Ha ha. What's it going to hurt for you to spend the night? Do you snore and think you'll keep me up all night?"

Rather than tell her the truth, he made something up. "Maybe I'm the one who won't be able to sleep."

"I don't *snore*."

"No, but you'll take up half the bed. And you're...hard to ignore. Sleeping seems like such a waste."

And there's the whole attachment thing. His now, not so much hers, it would seem. If she didn't have any worries she'd get too attached to him, she was in a very different place than he was at the moment. But mention that, and he had a feeling he'd be out on his ass too soon tonight for his taste. The buttery popcorn smell had now permeated the kitchen and almost overpowered her own sweet flowery scent. He brushed up against her and stopped the timer on the microwave.

"What are you doing?"

"It's going to burn. Never listen to the directions. Once the pops slow down, it's ready." Deliberately, his hand drifted from the small of her back and came to rest on her round ass.

She didn't pull away. "Are you some kind of a popcorn expert or something?"

"Or something." He grinned and kissed her neck, gratified by the hitch in her breath.

"You sure have a good way of distracting me."

"Why? Forget all about the popcorn?" he whispered as his hand dove under her robe and tweaked a soft nipple until it rose to a full peak.

"For now." She smiled against his lips.

Then for the second time that night, he carried her into the bedroom. As a compromise, he promised he wouldn't leave until she fell asleep. Predictably, he didn't doze off but instead stared at the numbers on the digital clock as he heard her breaths become slow and even. He asked himself again how in the hell he'd gotten into this predicament.

Where had he gone off track? Had it been the moment they met, when he'd recognized something of himself in her? Proud but fighting the shame she harbored. Feisty but vulnerable. Or maybe it had been the night on the beach when she'd spelled it out for him. Maybe it had been in Hollywood, when he'd taken her on that silly bus tour and acted like they were together.

He had no idea, but he did know one thing. He would have to get back on target soon. Like tomorrow. Close to the midnight hour, D.C. quickly dressed, hurrying to get to the main house before the locks went on. He jogged over, believing he'd make it.

But when he arrived at 11:59, the doors were locked.

15

"Mercy" by Brett Young

D.C. cursed a blue streak.

"It's not midnight," he argued with no one.

What the hell was he supposed to do now? He could go back to Sabrina, but he'd locked the door behind him, and he didn't want to wake her. Going back would also defeat the purpose of not spending the night in the first place. He felt like a kid who'd missed curfew.

Pulling on the door again, he wrenched on it hard, hoping someone inside might hear him and take pity. No one did. This was what he got for not staying at a hotel in town. The lobby doors stayed open all night instead of this mom-and-pop scenario.

"Stay at the Wilder B&B, I said. I'll save time, I said. Idiot!"

"Oh, hello," said a small voice behind him.

He turned and thanks to his awesome run of luck these days, he was ninety-nine percent sure this middle-aged blonde woman, who had green eyes a shade darker than her daughter's, was Kit Wilder. In the flesh. Time had done its work, and she looked different than the photos he'd seen of her on the Internet.

She was still a beautiful woman, though not dressed to the nines as in all the photos he'd seen of her. She wore worn jeans and a ratty looking sweater, her hair up in a ponytail. Not the normal style for the woman once called a fashionista by some in Nashville.

"Got locked out," D.C. said. "Traffic. Big pile-up on Highway 1."

She quirked a brow. "That's unusual at this time of the night. And...pretty much any night in Whistle Cove."

Bad lie, D.C., bad lie. "I'm Damien Caldwell. Everyone calls me D.C." He shook her hand.

"I've heard all about you." She moved to the side and a small mailbox where she removed a key. "I'll let you in."

The key had been right in front of him the entire time. "They keep a key there? Why? Isn't that dangerous?"

She smiled. "Not in Whistle Cove. Besides, sometimes our guests get in late even though they'd reserved a room for the night. We don't turn anyone away. All they need to do is call ahead, and Jessie leaves the key. It's old-fashioned self-service."

"That makes sense."

She unlocked the door, then slipped the key into her pants pocket. "I was out taking a late- night walk on the beach. It's so tranquil. Peaceful."

He could hear the rhythmic sounds of ocean waves crashing nearby. Soothing was another word. It helped him get to sleep some nights. The only bad thing about Texas was having only one coastline to the south. Hey, nobody and nothing was perfect. But Texas was damn near close.

"Thanks for letting me in," he said, holding the door open for her. "Guess I better hit the sack."

"That's okay," she said, not stepping inside with him. "I'm staying at my daughter's old cottage not far from Sabrina's."

Good thing he was leaving tomorrow as that proximity would definitely complicate everything. As if it wasn't already complicated enough. "Well...goodnight and thanks again."

He turned but her voice stopped him cold. "Actually, since you're here, and I'm here, it might be a good idea to talk." She stepped inside and shut the doors.

Seconds from a clean getaway! "About what?"

"My daughter, of course. Your plans for her. I hope they fit the image of the good girl she is at heart. I don't know what Rise Up Records wants from her, but she needs to get back to her roots. Her wholesome image. *That's* who she is at heart."

"I agree," he said, hoping to God it would be that simple, knowing deep down it wouldn't be.

"Would you like a glass of wine?" She smiled, already moving toward a bottle of wine left on the table.

"I've got to—"

"Just a quick one while we chat." She left the room and came back with two crystal glasses. Setting them down on the table near the fireplace, she poured for both of them.

He accepted the glass and did the usual observing of properties and smell, somewhat second nature to him now. And nicely distracting for the moment.

She noticed. "Do you know much about wine?"

"Not really," he confessed. "More of a Scotch guy. Sorry."

"Don't apologize to me," she said on a laugh. "I don't own the vineyard."

She took a seat on the leather couch by the fireplace, and he did the same, slipping into professional mode. "How can I ease your concerns about your daughter?"

"That's already been done. I've heard excellent things about you from Lexi, and I appreciate you coming here to help my daughter get back to what she was born to do."

He cleared his throat. "You should know, I've talked to Sabrina about whether the music industry is the right place for her."

"I'm sorry?" Kit furrowed her brow and went all narrowed eyes on him.

"Sabrina grew up in the business, so it was never her choice. She told me no one has ever asked her if performing is what she really wants."

He could almost feel the temperature drop in the room by a good twenty degrees. Frosty with a cold front coming in.

Kit's lips were a thin straight line. "My daughter was never *forced* to do anything she didn't want to do."

"Not what I meant. She's a grown woman now, no longer a kid, and she can choose for herself."

"Yes, she can *choose* to continue to do the only thing she's ever wanted to do. She sang before she could talk. I'd play songs in the car because she hated long car rides. The score from *The Lion King*, and she'd hum along. No words, because she was only a year old!"

"I don't doubt it." He would tell her how well he knew her daughter, and the fact that she'd even sang to him in bed tonight, but that was none of her business.

"With children, you don't always know what they will grow up to be. I had no idea that Lexi would be a songwriter, or that Jessie would have a knack for rhythm, but I knew from the moment I had Sabrina that she would be some-one...very special."

"I guarantee you she'll decide to stay in the business. But she needs to choose that life."

"Do you do this for all your clients?"

"No. But, as you said, Sabrina is...special."

"I'm so relieved to hear you say that. She's an innocent who was preyed on by an older man looking for a payday."

First time he'd heard the man in question referred to as an "older" man, and it grated on him. He was also older than Sabrina.

"Mrs. Wilder," he began.

"Kit—"

"This business, like so many other highly competitive careers, can be cut-throat at times. Sabrina won't have her sisters with her like she did before. She'll be traveling with a group of people selected by the label that signs her. Strangers. She's going to need to learn how to trust herself all over again and know that she can be a good judge of people."

"You're right, but I'm sure she will handle all of that. We will all help." She put her empty wine glass down. "I under-stand there's an interview with the press tomorrow."

He nodded. "The first time she'll tell her side of the story."

"I personally don't think *that's* such a good idea, and I wish you would have consulted with me first."

"I don't consult with anybody."

Kit straightened. "I'm her *mother*. What I think matters. Isn't it better to just forget the whole thing ever happened?"

"Well, that would be nice, sure. But it's not going to happen. The minute she's out among the media again, doing press junkets, the scandal will be brought up again. And again. Until it's dealt with."

"I'm afraid for her. Those awful reporters hurt her. If it happens again..."

"She's stronger than you realize."

"That doesn't mean we should feed her to the wolves."

It irritated him that she thought he would do that. He was here to prevent her being fed to the wolves.

"What you need to realize is that pretty soon this scandal will finally be behind you. It will be old news. Hiding out may have accomplished the purpose of taking a break, but this will resurface again. Better to get ahead of it. Trust me."

"But—"

He emptied his glass and set it down. "Goodnight, Kit. Thanks again for letting me in. Nice meeting you."

And with that, he turned from the suddenly silent Kit and went upstairs to his room. This time to sleep.

TODAY SABRINA WOULD FACE the big, bad media and tell her own story. Damien was right. She had to face this and finally give her side of the story, humiliating though it was. Therefore, she would put on her game face and deal. Just like she had when she'd been eleven and wanted to play with her Barbie, but Daddy had said it was time to practice. He'd been right. Practice made perfect, or close enough, and by the time she was fourteen, she could sing and dance like she'd been born to do it. Which maybe she had been. Or maybe it was just one of many things she could do with her life.

Sabrina wanted a family of her own someday, with children that she didn't want to force onto a tour bus with her. What then? Starting over scared her a little, too. She could be a flop at anything else she tried. But she wanted to get out on her own, away from the B&B, and feel like a real grown-up. Sometimes she thought that being this close to her family, both with work and life, had sheltered her too much from real life. Paying bills. Cleaning. Laundry. Having a long-term relationship that would last. Like her parents. That's what she wanted, too. But she'd wound up in a life-style where few couples got lucky with lasting love.

This was all so complicated and there was little time left to decide the rest of her life. No pressure.

There was a knock on her door, and Sabrina checked the time. It probably wasn't Damien as he'd told her he'd meet her just before the interview. The reporter was coming to them, and they would be using Jessie's private office so as not to disturb their guests.

Sabrina opened the door to find her mother on the other side. "Good morning, sweet girl."

"Hey. What's up?" She moved toward her bedroom. "I'm just laying out my clothes for the interview."

"Looks like I'm just in time."

Sabrina bristled at the comment. She was old enough to dress herself, thank you very much. Thanks to Damien and Luke, she now had an impressive wardrobe to choose from. Fortunately, the titty dress was hiding in the back of her closet, hoping for a special (ahem) occasion.

Sabrina waved at the selection on her bed. She also hadn't bothered to put out the blingy gown or other evening wear. "Lots of choices and all of them classy."

"This is your new wardrobe?" Mom picked up a black dress, one of Sabrina's favorites.

It said elegant and classy, all things she wanted to be. It

had capped sleeves, a sweetheart neckline, and tapered at the waist with a wide skirt. It came to just above her knees, so a little bit of sexy with the classy. She was leaning toward it for the interview and would wear it with her red stiletto pumps.

"Most of it."

Mom held the dress against Sabrina's body, and her eyes wandered to the skirt. "Cute but it's black."

"Black is always in."

"I always liked you wearing color. Pink, red, blue. Cheery."

Because she still thought of Sabrina as a child with a sunny disposition. And she was still that girl on some basic level. Except she'd grown up this past year, and she didn't always have to wear color. Black didn't mean she was depressed. It meant she knew who she was with or without the perfect color.

"I'm wearing this one." Sabrina took it from her mom, decision made.

Before her mom rendered her opinion, Sabrina had been on the fence. Was black too somber? Did this dress imply she'd been in mourning over her career? But no, this was *the* dress. She hoped that didn't make her childish, but she would start making decisions on her own from this point forward. Might as well start with the dress.

"At least wear some color with your shoes," Mom said, heading toward Sabrina's shoe collection.

"I'm wearing the red...boots." She'd just made that decision. Right this minute.

"Why not these red stilettos? Matches the style of the dress better." Mom held the strappy pumps in her hands.

"I don't want to match today." Sabrina held up the western boots, admiring them. They made her think of ranches and cowboys and a certain man who was under her skin. "I got these in Texas."

The outfit said, "I may look sophisticated but, actually, I'm country strong." No matter what she'd do with the rest of her life, country would stay in her blood. Forever. It was a state of mind as much as it was a music genre. She loved all of it *and* the hardcore fans. Every song told a story. Today she'd have one of her own to tell.

But because she was loyal to those she loved, some of it would remain unsaid. Her true story was one of a girl who'd never had a choice, and a girl who'd let people take care of her for too long. Her story was about a girl who'd been so sheltered that she wrongly assumed she could trust everyone.

Not anymore, and that was okay.

"At least let me help you with accessories." Mom went to the wall where Sabrina had her extensive collection of costume earrings and necklaces held up with simple push-pins. Hey, it worked.

"Sure. You decide."

Mom's eyes brightened. She just wanted to be needed, Sabrina told herself. Even if she wished her mom had moved home sooner, she was here now and that counted.

She held up red hoops to Sabrina's ears. "These would go well if you wear your hair up a little bit. These would be best if you wear it down."

Up and down they went from her ears, at least ten different dangly ones, until Mom finally decided on the red hoops. "Perfect."

"Thanks for moving back home," Sabrina said, thinking it was time to be honest. "I wish you had sooner, but I'm happy now."

Mom's eyes got leaky. "I wish I had too, honey, but this

town reminds me too much of John. It's where we met and fell in love. Where we started our family. We were so young and had such big dreams. He's everywhere I turn, and it hurts so much."

"I miss him, too. But we have each other. You have daughters, and we all need you. Even Jessie does."

"You're right. I'm here now, and I'll do anything you need me to do. Your manager, your agent, whatever you need."

"It's okay, Mom. I just want you to be my mother. What I need you to do is stay here with Jessie and Gran and help with the B&B. This is where you're really needed."

"If you don't need me, that's fine. But at least listen to me. I'm worried about this interview." She pulled on Sabrina's arms and shook her gently.

"Damien has only allowed the reporter to ask me pre-approved questions."

"Speaking of *that man*, he's very arrogant. I don't think I like him."

Sometimes it hit Sabrina square between the eyes that she really was her mother's daughter. Her thoughts clearly echoed her own before she'd gotten to know and understand the man. It wasn't arrogance. His was a confidence that poured out of him. The knowledge that he was his own man. He'd made his way in the world with the help of no one. He didn't need anyone. Very different from her and yet so much like her in some ways.

"He's all right once you get to know him."

"I don't like this at all. He said you're going to have to talk about The Scandal."

"It's time I did. Now my fans can listen to my side of the story. I bet you anything there's another girl out there who's trusted someone she shouldn't have. Maybe I can help her realize her life doesn't have to be over because of that."

This meant more to Sabrina than she'd ever thought it could. She'd learned a tough lesson and very publicly, but somewhere there was another girl who might be suffering her own humiliation a lot more privately.

Mom worried a fingernail between her teeth. "I wish your father was here. He'd know what to do."

"Mom, *I* know what to do. And I think he would have done this, too, only sooner. He wouldn't have let us hide out in shame."

"It's about closing ranks and taking care of each other when you don't know who else you can trust. It's not about shame!"

"It will seem that way unless I talk about all this. Unless I make it clear I'm holding my head up. Unless I let them know that no one's ever going to take me down again."

16

"Body like a Backroad" by Sam Hunt

Sabrina thought the reporter seemed very nice. Felicia Tyler had her credentials from *Country Scene.* She was tall and slim, with jet black hair cut in an angular and trendy fashion. She was beautiful with coffee-colored eyes that seemed very attuned to Damien. Not that Sabrina was preoccupied with this. Felicia had brought along a photographer, too, and he took photos of Sabrina both sitting and standing on the deck outside. A few of her inside the B&B. She'd been assured final approval on all photos before publication.

"Thank you," Felicia now said to Sabrina as she sat behind Jessie's desk. "Damien owed me a favor, but I'm still grateful that you've allowed me to tell your side of the story. For a year, your fans have wanted to hear from you. And now they finally will."

"I'm happy to share the truth." Sabrina folded her jerky hands on her lap and forced them to be still.

Damien stood in the doorframe of Jessie's office, arms

folded, quietly listening. His eyes were their usual dark intensity as they zeroed in on everything at once. Each time Felicia asked a question, even though Sabrina had been prepped, she still glanced at him for reassurance. No idea why. He'd nod almost imperceptibly, and the rock in the pit of her stomach would roll away. She was doing well. Acing this. Even though Damien was leaving on a flight tonight for Dallas, Sabrina was relieved in a way. It was good to get everything out in the open, like a boulder lifted off her heart. She only wished she'd done this sooner. Truth was a powerful thing.

Damien's phone rang, and he flexed his index finger, meaning the interview would pause. He walked away with the phone to his ear.

"He's very protective of you, isn't he?" Felicia asked.

"I'm sure he's like that with all of his clients. How did you two meet?"

She tossed her hair back. "D.C. and I go way back. I had a little crush on him. I helped him out, now he's helping me out. Quid pro quo. Plus, we had a little something-something once or twice. Didn't last long. That's who he is. Not the settling down type."

Sabrina swallowed hard, her face burning. Felicia sure was forthcoming, and Sabrina had heard more than she'd wanted to.

If you don't want to know, don't ask.

He'd lied to her, just like she'd heard him lie to other people to make her sound better. It was obviously not the only reason he lied. She *wasn't* the first person with whom he'd crossed professional and ethical lines. There was probably a whole lot of other lies he'd told her. All things she didn't want to think about right now.

"What you about you and D.C.?" Felicia glanced at the

door, which was still unoccupied by his frame. "Off the record, I mean."

Off the record or not, Sabrina had learned her lesson well. "Damien and I have a professional relationship, and we've also become good friends."

Never truer than today. She was better off without him, and she knew this. They didn't want the same things out of life. He wanted Texas and life on a ranch. She wasn't entirely sure what she wanted yet, though she was leaning toward going back to Nashville, where she could still do good things like charity work to help animals. Like start her own fashion line, with help from her mom, who would love that. What she didn't want in any lifetime was manure and lowing cows. She was better off, so why did her heart feel like it had been dropkicked across the floor? Why were her hands trembling?

Because she was stupid, that's why.

The devil's son appeared in the doorway again and nodded that they could resume the interview. Sabrina finished her "statement," took a breath, and got ready for more questions.

"I'm sorry that happened to you," Felicia said, and she sounded as if she meant it.

"My mistake, entirely."

"Not actually. The dude's an idiot. What he did was so unfair. We women have to stick together, don't we?"

"Uh-huh," Sabrina said, not feeling the ground solid beneath her boots for a moment. Where was this going?

"What is your response to the fact that he's shopping a story to *Tell Me!* He's saying now that he was married at the time, and you knew this when you began the relationship."

Sabrina froze, and tiny black specks floated before her eyes. *Married.* That wasn't...possible. "I...I don't..."

Why was this happening, and *why* had Damien allowed this question without preparing her for it? He'd allowed her to be blindsided with this information. The simple answer was that, like others, he'd betrayed her, too. She turned to face him and glare him right into next month. But as she did, his hand was on her arm, pulling her up from the seat.

"This interview is over."

"Wait." Felicia stood up. "You promised me an exclusive. Am I supposed to ignore the latest? If it's not true, she can simply deny it."

"You knew our deal." Damien had his hand on the small of Sabrina's back and moved her swiftly through the doorway.

"Please." Felicia followed them out. "Let me explain."

"I threw you a bone," Damien said, a fierce tone in his voice she'd never heard before. "We're done here."

Relief that he hadn't known about the question was quickly followed by outright panic. What would her fans think of her now? Everyone hated a cheater. She hated cheaters. Cheating was unforgivable. A cheater was practically the lowest form of life on earth. She continued to move in a half daze as Damien led her down the hallway and up the steps toward his room. It was the closest available for privacy. He opened the door, and she found herself tugged inside.

Sabrina was still having a difficult time breathing. When Damien finally let go of her, she grabbed his forearm. "It's not true...it can't be...I didn't know. You believe me, don't you?"

He tipped her chin and met her eyes. "Look at me, Sunshine. Breathe."

"But I...I...you have to know."

"I have to know only one thing right now. That you can

breathe. Slow and even."

She slowed, purposely breathing in and out, conscious of every single breath. No other thoughts were allowed inside her head. Just the breathing. It was all she could manage at the moment.

Damien folded her into his arms and held on tightly. He kissed the top of her head. "That's my girl. You have to know that question wasn't on the list. A cheap shot. I would never have allowed it. Believe that."

"I do," she said into his warm button-down shirt. "Because you were so pissed."

"No one fucks with me," he growled.

"She did," Sabrina said. "Why did she do that to you?"

"No idea, except that she knows I'm on my way out of this business. Probably figured she had nothing to lose. Didn't think it through because I still have connections. I can still cut her out."

"Maybe she's jealous."

He pulled back to meet her eyes, hand at the nape of her neck. "Of *what*?"

"Of you, dummy. She said you two had a little some-thing-something once," Sabrina said as she held up finger quotes. "But that since you're not the settling down type—"

"I never had anything to do with her that wasn't purely professional. I meant it when I told you I'd never crossed the line before you."

Relief took a slow slide down her spine. "She lied about that. What else is she lying about?"

"Should have seen her for the complete opportunist that she is. I'm off my game, that's for damn sure." He stepped away from her, pacing the length of the room.

For the first time, she took a serious look around. The bed was made, corners tucked in perfectly. Blanket smoothed down with not a wrinkle on it. He had a few items on hangers, his laptop on the table by the TV. Everything in place. Meticulous.

"What are we going to do?" She sat on the edge of his bed.

"You're not going to do anything." He pointed to her. "You're going to relax and know that I've got this under control. Got a few phone calls to make. A flight to cancel, and—"

A flight to cancel.

"You're going to stay?" Hope crashed through her, rolling in waves. She'd have more time with him.

"I have to stay and take care of this situation. There's no way this joke of a story is getting published. Anywhere. You heard her. He's trying to shop it to the rags. There could be no truth to the story. Bet he's not even married, or if he is, he wasn't then. And we can prove that. He's an idiot if he thinks he'll even sell to the tabloids. They do *some* fact checking, at least."

"Why does anyone even still care about this?" There were so many other scandals. Many were far more salacious than hers, even if she'd known the guy was married which she had not. She hoped to God he was lying because even without knowing, if it turned out to be true, she would need to take thirty showers in a row. At least.

He stopped pacing and sat beside her. "Because people like to throw dirt at things that shine. And like it or not, by keeping quiet all this time, the fire of rumor and innuendo has been stoked by imagination. Who knows why, but it's fascinating to watch someone so special take a fall. Trip. They expect it out of some people and are not surprised when it happens again and again. But with you, they're shocked. Seeing someone like you make a mistake makes them feel human. If you're allowed to make a mistake, then maybe so can they."

"But...if the tabloids believe him and buy his story...will this hurt any contract offers?"

"I doubt it. There's so much interest now and this might even spur record sales."

"I don't want to be known as a home-wrecker, Damien. I'm no Jolene. My fans will hate me if they think I am. I don't care how many records I sell if my loyal fans hate me."

"And that's why you're special." He tweaked her chin.

"I hate these lies. And I don't know how special I am when I'm not sure if this is what I want to do with the rest of my life."

He studied her solemnly. "Maybe that's because you've already been doing it."

"Working at the B&B?" She wrinkled her nose.

"No, baby. Singing. You've been doing it all your life. Just because you didn't choose that life doesn't mean you can't choose it now. It's who you are."

He was right. Nothing excited her as much as music did. Nothing ever had. It didn't make any sense to fight it. For her it was more than a job. It was who she was at her core. She couldn't let a few nasty people decide for her.

"You're one of the lucky ones who finds out early what they're going to be doing with the rest of their life. And gets to do it."

She knew that was true. "But I want other things, too. Like a man in my life. And, maybe someday, even a baby. Or two."

He was quiet for a minute. "And you'll have it, if that's what you want."

"Will I?"

"Any man would be lucky."

"All I'm going to meet are people in the music business. And I'm going to need a man in my life who doesn't need me to help advance his career. Who doesn't want my fame to rub off on him."

What she was really saying, on some level, was that she wanted a man just like Damien. He was a cowboy for crying out loud. With plenty of his own money. What on earth could she do for him? Problem being, what on earth could she *do* for him? That cut sliced both ways.

"Don't worry about any of that right now."

"What about the ranch? I don't want you to lose it."

"Believe me, I won't." He rose and strode to the door. "Stay here for a bit while I check that the coast is clear."

"No. I'm done hiding, Damien. I did that for a year." She stood up and smoothed the skirt of her dress. "I don't care whether they're gone or not."

Hand on the doorknob, he stared at her with a mixture of surprise and confusion. "Do you want to address this now? Or should we give the story to someone else? I didn't like her blindsiding us."

That was sweet. She kind of liked the way he used "us" instead of "you." But even if it might mean he'd leave tonight anyway, she wanted to take care of this and get it behind her. It was just as Damien had explained. Get in front of it before it can do too much damage.

"I guess she was just doing her job." Though she hated the lie concerning Damien. What else would she lie about? "Do you think she'd print exactly what I tell her?"

"If we have a recording of the conversation, she could lose her job if she doesn't."

"Then let's do this." Sabrina strode to the door. "I have my side of this story to tell, and she's here now. I want to get my truth out there and the sooner the better."

17

"Taking Back My Brave" by Carolyn Dawn Johnson

The kid was amazing. No. Not a kid. Not even "Sunshine." He was going to have to come up with another nickname. Because Sabrina was a woman, and she'd proved it today. Hell, she'd taken his advice even when *he* hadn't. He was definitely off his game. Outraged and fiercely protective over her, he'd acted uncharacteristically. He was still pissed that Felicia would ignore his request, but now that she'd brought it up, they'd get in front of it. She was right.

His feelings when he'd heard the question ranged from outrage to something that felt too uncomfortably like jealousy. Pure and simple. This guy continued to insert himself into Sabrina's life like an obsessed fan, or a spurned lover. Damien almost hoped he was simply after a payday, and not that his actions would escalate into stalker behavior. Always a possibility. He led the way, Sabrina following, as they walked back downstairs to the common area. Not surprisingly, Felicia sat at a table typing furiously into her phone.

She glanced up as he approached and executed an almost comical double-take.

Putting her phone down, she stood. "Don't worry. I just called an Uber."

"Still want that interview?" D.C. said, putting steel in his voice. "Sabrina wants to do it."

"She does?" Felicia smiled at Sabrina, now at his elbow. "That's...that's great."

"You should know this thing about the guy claiming he was married is absolutely new to her," D.C. said.

"I had no idea," Sabrina now said. "That's why I was so shocked."

"Well, she wouldn't have been had she not been blind-sided." D.C. put his arm around Sabrina.

"I apologize," Felicia said. "I don't like this style of guer-rilla journalism, but sometimes it's the only thing that works."

"I'm not doing this for your readers," Sabrina said. "I'm doing it for my fans."

D.C. pulled Felicia aside. "Ask her your questions, but unless his story is actually sold to a tabloid, keep it all off the record. And you keep in mind this man continues to try and insert himself into her life. You and your organization do not want to encourage stalker-like behavior I'm going to assume. You could be liable."

She blinked, as if only now considering the possibility. "You're right."

When he turned to Sabrina, she stared from him to Felicia and back again. Her eyes were questioning, narrowed suspiciously. Yeah, jealousy. He got that, since a similar emotion had coursed through him only a few minutes ago. Irrational of both of them. D.C. had now missed three calls from his real estate agent and two from a record label executive. He had things to do.

Choosing to reassure her more than he cared about what anyone else thought, D.C. put his hand on the nape of her neck. He bent down to whisper in her ear. "Do you need me, baby?"

Giving him a smile he'd come to anticipate like the sunrise, she shook her head. "I'm fine."

Back in his room, he called his travel agent to cancel his flight and chose not to reschedule right away. With some trepidation, he returned the call to his real estate agent to hear the latest.

"I asked around. The Farrells are not huge fans of the senior Mr. Caldwell."

Was anyone? His biological father seemed hell bent on owning all the cattle in Texas. Not going to happen.

"I've got amazing news. They've accepted your first offer. All I have to do is start escrow on my end. I'll have an offer letter faxed, and you need to sign and get it back to me. We'll take care of all the official paperwork and contract when you get here. The ranch will be yours, D.C."

Suddenly, it hit him.

They knew. Even if he wasn't one of the Dallas Caldwells, they'd found his association. It probably didn't take a private investigator to figure this out, but Texas was huge. Plenty of Caldwells, most of whom were no relation.

"That's...that's the best news I've had all day."

"D.C., they knew your mother. Their daughter was her friend and worked with her at the golf course."

Even in a place as large and populated as Dallas, someone had made the connection without any help from him. It was going to be a kick in the nuts when his father learned he'd taken the ranch from him without having to match the offer. He wished he could see the old man's face when he got the news.

Now he had another phone call to make. This one to one of the few friends he had in the world. He had a little favor to ask his old football buddy, Mick. He now owned a full-service, high-level security agency that he'd built into a multi-million-dollar company.

"Yo, D.C. Long time no talk."

"Got a favor to call in." He hadn't asked for many from Mick over the years, and, in fact, had helped him find funding when he'd first started out.

D.C. explained the situation. He wanted the man who was trying to shop this possibly bogus story to the tabloids checked out. Marriages, financial records, criminal records.

"You want I should pay him a little visit?" Mick asked in his best Al Pacino impersonation.

But D.C. wasn't in the mood. "Just do it, Mick. Check this guy out for me. Get back to me ASAP."

"Done."

D.C. hung up and made his way back downstairs to check on the interview but ran into Jessie Wilder.

She beckoned him into her private office and shut the door. Then she handed him a fax. "Got it early this morning."

The fax was from the largest recording label in Nashville. A deal memo. He quickly scanned it. They wanted Sabrina and wanted her immediately. If she accepted their offer, she was to be in Nashville within a week to sign the contract and go into the studio to record. They wanted this forwarded to her agent, because they'd found no record of her representation.

Jessie stared at him with crossed arms. "Is that what I think it is?"

"It is. It sure is." He read it again to be certain.

"She needs an agent. I'm guessing you're not going to do that for her, too?" Jessie's eyes narrowed. She looked so much like her little sister at that moment that it was a little disconcerting.

"She might want to sign with Lexi's agency."

"That would be best. Don't let my mother know, or she'll try to be Sabrina's agent and mess everything up by asking for too much."

At this point, he was fairly certain Sabrina could ask for just about anything. The offer was generous and came with a signing bonus. One caveat: she would sign a four-year exclusive with them and give up creative control. He had no idea if that was normal, but a good agent would know and be able to negotiate on her behalf.

"I'll let Sabrina know the good news, and she can phone the agency and start the process." He thanked Jessie and turned to go.

She stopped him. "Wait."

"Yeah?"

"Sabrina calls you Damien. Not D.C. You two spent some time together, and I've seen the way you look at her. Don't worry, I know it's mutual. But Sabrina has never been able to turn away a handsome man. I hope you know that."

Busted. Yeah, he shouldn't be surprised Jessie knew about them, but he could hope that she was the only one who'd noticed. As a close sister, she'd be finely tuned in. But he didn't appreciate being lumped in with all the other "handsome" men she'd met.

"Anything else?" he asked, biting his tongue, unwilling to share with the class.

"Don't hurt her. She might look like she's got a tough shell, and she puts up a good act, but she's gooey on the inside. And she's been hurt so much this last year that I can't stand to see anyone else hurting her. For *any* reason."

Precisely why he hadn't wanted to start anything with her. He'd seen that soft and tender underbelly. She was strong, sure, but that didn't mean her heart couldn't be easily touched. "You don't have to worry. We have an understanding."

It was as far as he'd share.

Jessie's eyebrow quirked in surprise. He understood that Sabrina had probably never had this kind of a situation with a man before. But he'd tried to stay away from her. She wouldn't quit, and he'd made his situation clear enough for her. Still, the knowledge that he'd hurt her churned in his gut. Maybe it was time to stop this thing between them. They both had contracts that would take them in very different directions.

And if these contracts weren't a metaphor for their relationship, he honestly didn't know what was.

SABRINA THOUGHT the rest of the interview with Felicia went well. She felt so good about it that she wanted to celebrate. Finding Damien seemed like a good way to begin. She went back to his room and knocked. The door opened slowly, and when Damien turned immediately to walk away from her, she half expected to find him on a phone call. But he walked to the small two-chair table by the windows and held up an unopened bottle of champagne. He gave her a slow smile when her eyes went to the bottle, then him, and back to the bottle.

"Good news?" she asked. "Did you get the ranch?"

"Yeah," he said, and popped the cork.

Excitement pulsed through her. She jumped in the air and did a jig. "Yay, cowboy!"

He held up the foaming bottle. "It might be a little early in the day for this."

"Not at all. We serve mimosas three times a year before noon: Mother's Day, Father's Day, and New Year's Day."

"Too bad we don't have orange juice." He poured the bubbles into wine glasses from their wine tasting. "I may have taken these."

She came up behind him, wrapped her arms around his waist, and hugged him tight. "I'm so happy for you."

This was the best news she could have received today. Damien hadn't had an easy life, and now he'd get to retire to his dream. She couldn't be happier for him.

"You're going to be happy for yourself in a second."

"Oooh, *that* sounds intriguing." She licked her lips.

"I do love the way your mind works." He turned and handed her a glass. "And even though I love that you went there, this is about you."

"I know it is," she teased. "You always make sure it's about me. At least twice."

He slid her a smug look. "You have an offer. And it's a good one."

"I have an offer? *Me*?"

"From the largest label in Nashville. They want you back in Nashville in a week or sooner."

She didn't know what else to do, so she dropped to the closest surface, which was his bed, holding her champagne glass. "That was fast."

"You need an agent. I'm going to suggest you sign with Lexi's agency."

"That's...that's a good idea. I'll call her." Even her mom would be happy with that outcome.

Damien clinked his glass with hers. "To your comeback."

"To my comeback," she said.

She should be happier. This was what she wanted. For the first time in a long while, she felt safe enough to go back to Nashville. Lexi was there. Sabrina had learned how to face accusations and not hide from them. She'd found a good way to tell her story. One that didn't make her sound like a stupid kid. She was still holding her full glass, and Damien was now studying her.

"Sunshine. What's wrong?"

"Nothing." She went ahead and downed it. The sugary sweet bubbles went down smoothly. "More, please."

He poured and sat beside her on the bed. "Thought you'd be happier."

"I am, but I think all the news is a little much. You hit me with it all at once. I fully expected to celebrate your ranch."

"We're doing both."

"To your ranch." She held up her glass and met his.

"Thanks, baby."

"What happened?"

"Turns out, these people don't want to sell to my father. They took my first offer."

"You mean you don't have to match his offer?"

He shook his head. "I can afford to match the offer. Of course, it would set me back. And there's nothing I hate worse than paying more than fair market value."

"Maybe they're decent people who don't want someone to take the ranch away from you just because he can."

"They knew my mother."

He said it so plainly and with such a flat tone that anyone else might believe it didn't matter. Sabrina knew it did. His eyes had taken on a very different shine the two times he'd mentioned her. As someone who understood pain and shame, who'd lived there, she recognized it well.

She set her glass down and crawled onto his lap. "Baby."

"It's okay. It was a long time ago."

"You won." She threaded her fingers through his thick dark hair. "Enjoy it."

"As soon as you do."

"Sorry, but I can't enjoy the fact that you're leaving."

"Not now I'm not." His arms tightened around her. "I just have to wire the money and escrow starts. I'll sign papers when I get back next week."

"We have a week."

"I have a week. Not sure if *you* have a week."

"Oh, I have a week." She wiggled on his lap. "After all this time, you better believe I'm going to make sure my agent reviews the contract. Negotiates it if she has to. I'm not going to rush into a contract that isn't the best one I can get. No one's going to own me."

A slow smile slid across his handsome face and made her womb contract. "Damn, but you're sexy when you talk business to me."

"Oh, yeah?"

"I like an ambitious woman. It's not a dirty word, you know. For men or women."

A sense of pride swept through her, filling her lungs, and she felt like a peacock about to spread her wings. "Thank you for that. It's nice to be in charge for the first time in my life."

"You are in charge, and don't you forget it. You call the shots." Warm, strong hands slid down her arms and cuffed her wrists.

"And don't you forget it."

Taking her cue, she pushed him down on the bed with

one hand. She knew he went back easily because he wanted to, and not because she was physically strong enough to do this. That made it even sexier.

"But we should probably stop this now."

She stopped moving as an icicle slid over her heart. "Do you *want* to stop?"

He'd given her no indication that he wanted to so much as slow down. Either she was reading him wrong, or something had happened. She already knew he was leaving, but, if anything, they now had more time. Unless he thought that time would invest her. She had news for him because she was already invested. In her own happiness. He made her happier than she'd been in one long and dry year.

"Hell, no. But your sister knows about us."

"Oh." Sabrina shouldn't be surprised that Jessie would intervene. She'd be worried about Sabrina because she hadn't been honest and open enough. She'd have to correct that soon.

"She caught me earlier, and we talked. She's noticed the way I look at you. Knows that you have a crush on me, as you do with most men who give you any attention."

There was so much information for her loaded in those sentences. *The way he looks at me. Do I crush on most men who give me attention?* No, she didn't. She had a pile of fan mail to prove it. Damien was special to her. Unique.

"I don't have a *crush* on you. And I don't crush on all men who give me attention." She stuck out her lower lip comically.

He smirked. "*That's* what you got out of what I just said?"

She clasped both of his hands above him and threaded her fingers through his. "I don't want you to think you're not special to me because you are."

His gaze softened. "Your sister knows about us."

"That's not a problem. Jessie has my back. If she gives me any grief, I can handle her."

"Does she have my back, Sunshine?"

She nodded. "I do, and that's what matters. And why do you call me Sunshine, anyway?"

"You're finally asking." Hands on her butt, he moved her right over his bulge. "Because you're bright and very hot."

"That's a great line."

He scowled. "Don't need a line. It's the truth."

Given the way he commanded a room with his presence, paired with his looks, he'd probably never needed a line with any woman. Ever. Certainly, he hadn't needed one with her. In fact, he'd been an ass. Pissed her off. And then Hollywood had happened, and she'd met a man she hadn't known existed under all that swagger and muscle.

"We have something to celebrate. Actually, two things." With that, she climbed off the bed and unzipped her dress, letting it fall to the floor.

He went up on his elbows, a wolfish smile on his face. "Leave the boots on."

18

"Follow Your Arrow" by Kacey Musgraves

A couple of hours later, Sabrina closed the door to the Sea Captain's Room and smoothed down her hair. Hoo boy. It seemed like the daylight hours gave the man extra stamina or something.

"Hello, dear," said a woman's voice from behind her.

Eileen.

Sabrina jumped away from the door. "I was just...just... changing the sheets in here and putting in fresh towels."

She said this even though she was sadly without a maid cart and wearing what came down to a party dress.

"What else would you be doing?" Eileen who apparently wasn't too observant, held up a small plate of pastries in one hand, coffee in the other. "I'm taking Jeff breakfast in bed this morning. Got to keep the flame alive."

"Great idea." Sabrina waved to Eileen as she kept walking.

She should do that, too. Bring Damien breakfast in bed. Though, they didn't have to worry about keeping a flame alive. Instead, they were going to have to put it out soon. Tamp it out. Watch it flicker and die until there was no fire left. Ugh! She refused to think about it anymore.

They had a week. Seven days and six nights, and she'd take advantage of every single minute.

She headed to her cottage to shower and change. Now *she* had phone calls to make. Things to do. People to see. She opened the door and nearly had a stroke.

"Jessie! Would you quit doing that?"

"Quit doing *what*? Looking out for you? Saving your butt? Having your back?" She crossed her arms and gave her a pissy look. "Which of these do you want me to stop doing?"

"Just...quit breaking and entering, yeah?"

"I'm not breaking and entering! I have a key." She held up her mega keyring set that had the key to every room at the B&B and probably some others, too.

"It's *my* place." She pouted and headed to the kitchen.

"Have you called Lexi with the news yet?" Jessie followed.

"No, but I will." She put a pod in the coffee machine. "Good news, huh?"

"Fantastic news. I hope you sign right away."

"I'm not going to *sign* until I know it's a good deal." She rummaged through her fridge for the creamer.

"Are you crazy? Sign before they change their mind!"

"I don't think so. I'm in control now. I'm in the driver's seat."

Jessie looked thoroughly confused. For a year, she'd probably thought Sabrina would jump at the chance to take any way back into Nashville. Everyone had.

"That's what Damien said," Sabrina reiterated. "I'm in charge."

"Ah, Damien. You mean the guy you're sleeping with even after I warned you not to?" Jessie grabbed Sabrina by the shoulders and shook. "You're going to get hurt, and no amount of heavy lifting on my part is going to fix that."

"You don't have to fix me, Jess. I know you're worried, but I've got this."

"Look me in the eye and tell me you're not totally invested in this guy."

"I'm not totally invested in this guy." She wouldn't meet Jessie's eyes.

"You have to *mean* it."

Sabrina threw up her hands in frustration. "And by the way, I wish you hadn't told him that I'm a sucker for *any* guy who gives me a little attention."

"No, this is just the first guy you've been with since The Scandal, so I would think you'd be a little cautious."

"I *am* cautious. And discreet."

"With your heart?"

All her life, she and her sisters had been drilled: guard your heart. Build a fortress around it. Put in a moat. Guard. Your. Heart. Her parents had wanted to protect her and her sisters from those who would take advantage of them. Those who craved a little bit of their fame. But they'd protected Sabrina, at least, too well. She'd never developed the skills she needed to learn how to trust someone on her own. She had them now.

"You don't get it. I trust him. That's new to me."

"It's not new to you. You trusted far too easily, that was your problem."

"Yeah, but then I didn't trust anyone at all. For a year. I know I need to trust someone besides you guys. Otherwise, I'll always be stuck."

"Why would you start with him above all people? You

hated him, you said so yourself."

"I changed my mind."

"But why? Just because he's hot?"

"No. Because...he can be tender, and he understands what it's like to feel ashamed. To have something terrible happen and need someone's help. I feel like he really 'sees' me, you know? He reminded me that I'm powerful and strong. All things I forgot for a while. And...and he took good care of me when he didn't have to."

"And by taking care of you, you mean—"

She stomped her foot. "I don't mean sex!"

"Well, excuse me for thinking that." Jessie rolled her eyes.

"Sex isn't the only thing that matters to me, you know. I care that a man is strong but tender. Someone who takes care of me even though he knows that I can take care of myself."

Jessie just stared slack-jawed. Sabrina didn't much care for that look, so she kept talking.

"All right, so maybe I light up when he walks into a room, but you don't need to worry because he's leaving. He bought a cattle ranch in Texas. And I'm okay with that because I want him to have it. He deserves it, and I need him to be happy."

"Oh, my God. This is far worse than I thought," Jessie said, palming her face. "You're in love with him."

"No, I'm not."

"Yes, yes, you are!"

"No! I'm not." Sabrina didn't want to believe this, but the moment Jessie said it out loud, it had a ring of truth to it. A trickle of fear slid down her spine.

"Brina," Jessie said softly.

No one but Jessie called her by that nickname anymore.

Not since she was a fourteen-year-old, curious about boys, but never having much a chance to get to know anyone. Receiving letters from heartsick boys who loved her from a distance. It had all been so confusing.

Sabrina felt a stirring deep in her stomach, rising slowly through her lungs, stealing all the oxygen. She felt her lower lip tremble and bit it fiercely to stop both it and the tears that formed. She couldn't do casual. Just wasn't designed for it. But Damien had made it clear. He wouldn't fall in love. It wasn't his fault her heart hadn't quite listened.

Jessie took Sabrina in her arms and hugged tight. "You can't keep your heart out of this."

"I know," she admitted and felt the warmth of Jessie's hug slice through her. "Hey, at least I have you."

"And Lexi. And Gran. And Mom. Olga and Tony. You will always have us."

"I'll be okay." Sabrina wasn't going to say something stupid and cliché like she was better off loving and losing than not loving him at all. None of that crap was true. She would not be better off. She didn't want to lose him. She didn't *want* to love him.

Where did that leave her?

She wondered if there was a cliché for that.

IN THE GOOD NEWS DEPARTMENT, the next day Sabrina learned that Lexi's agency was more than happy to take over her representation. Luke and Lexi would be setting out on a multi-city tour the following summer. Due to his huge success with his and Lexi's number one song, it would be his first time headlining. They both wanted Sabrina and her new back-up band to open for Luke.

Her new band.

A bunch of complete strangers. She was just a little bit petrified. Lexi's suggestion was a little premature, though, because Sabrina's agent had reviewed the contract and had some issues. One of those being creative control. Sabrina was going to kick back and enjoy what little time she had left at the B&B and in Whistle Cove. She'd traveled the world, and there was still nowhere like Monterey Bay. She would miss the ocean waves lulling her to sleep every night. She would miss Gran, Jessie, and Mom. But she was going to have to go to Nashville because she'd been born to do this. This was her life, this would be her future, and she couldn't regret it. She was a lucky woman to do what she loved for a living.

Unable to sleep, she rose early and took a walk along their private access beach. She sang "Follow Your Arrow" by one of her favorite singers. And it was exactly what she had to do. Follow her own path and not get distracted by one super-hot cowboy next door. She'd been avoiding him for a day, nursing her wounds at realizing she'd failed to keep her heart guarded. Unwilling to tell him she was a sensitive girl, a "kid" as he'd first called her, who wasn't mature enough to do the casual thing. But she'd also realized something about herself. She didn't ever want to be sophisticated enough to be that woman.

So there.

She walked along the beach, watching the pelicans fly over the salty ocean spray in search of a rock to land on. A sand dollar revealed itself from under grains of sand, and she bent to pick it up. These were rare, and she'd never found an unbroken one. She would count this as a good omen.

"To my brand-new life," she whispered and admired it.

"What are you doing up so early?" a deep and sultry voice called out over the comforting waves.

That lulling sense of calm she'd had seconds ago evaporated like the mist. Her heart kicked up like it always did when *he* walked into a room. Or when she saw him jogging, or when he was thrusting into her, his gaze so open and vulnerable. He'd been jogging, and his windswept hair curled around his ears, giving him an almost boyish look.

"I couldn't sleep." She kept walking, eyes on the ground searching for another sand dollar.

Pushing her luck, she realized, but what the heck. Where there was one, there might be two.

He slowed to keep in step with her. "What's happening with the contract?"

She told him the latest because they hadn't talked since the agency offered representation. "Who knows? I might be leaving right after you."

"Proud of you. You're going to be a superstar someday."

"I don't want to be a superstar." Those people didn't get to control their own lives. Now that she'd taken her life back, she wasn't willing to give it away again.

"You might not be able to help that."

"But I *will* help it. I'm in charge. Just like you said."

"That's right." He took her hand. "You been avoiding me, Sunshine?"

Her hand stiffened in his. "Ha! Avoiding? Aren't you the sensitive one?"

"Am I?"

"What? No one ever called you sensitive before? Does it offend your cowboy ways?" Too freaking bad, she wanted to say.

He could take it like a man. Or a rancher. Whatever.

"Hey." He stopped walking and pulled her to a stop beside him. "Didn't sleep well, either."

"Why not?" she asked softly. "Is your contract not everything you wanted?"

"Never mind about that," he growled. "I missed you."

"Really?"

"Yeah, of course." Fingers in the belt loop of her jeans, he tugged her close. "I only have a few more days here in paradise."

Right. And she hadn't wanted to waste any of those days and nights, either. Now she was wondering if she could afford to spend them with him.

"Got news," he said, hand on the nape of her neck. "I had a good friend of mine who owns a security company check out your guy."

She knew who he was referring to. "He's not my *guy*."

"I meant the idiot who sold the photo. He's married now, but he wasn't at the time."

Relief slid through her and she smiled. "Thank God."

"He's had a lot of financial trouble. It's doubtful he'll be able to sell his story, but if he does, it will be to one of the papers that covers important stories like Bigfoot sightings and UFO landings. No one will believe it. Plus, you're ready for him."

"I am. Thanks to you."

He tugged her close and kissed her softly on the lips. Even that small touch ignited a fire in her which spiked down her spine. "Are you busy tonight?"

She should stay away before she fell any deeper for him. On the other hand, maybe this whole thing between them couldn't possibly get any worse for her than it already was.

She was already so far down the rabbit hole that a few more nights with him weren't going to make a difference.

19

"I Could Use a Love Song" by Maren Morris

This right here is one stupid cowboy, D.C. told himself. It would be much easier to take the easy way out and let Sabrina ignore him. Only a few more days left. Much easier to spend the rest of his nights planning the operations of a full-time cattle ranch. He had his work cut out for him there to be certain. But with Sabrina, this somehow wasn't quite out of sight and out of mind. Then there was the fact that he'd found her walking along the beach collecting seashells and sand dollars. Yeah, and singing. To no one.

Fuck, he was going to miss that.

He was going to miss a whole lot about her. She'd handled his anti-social ways in the beginning. Somehow she'd gotten him to talk about his painful past when no one else had in recent history. He didn't know how she managed to pull him in because he was experienced enough to know this wasn't about the sex. Though, sure, hell yeah, the sex was amazing. Incredible. The best he'd ever had. Since she was younger and less experienced, he knew it all came down to their combustible chemistry. And her enthusiasm. She had that in spades.

Had he mentioned how much he'd miss her?

But tonight would be for her. All for her. A night where he'd play with her the way he'd wanted to in Hollywood. And more. He'd been preoccupied with his own image, carefully crafted over the years. A businessman above reproach. Ethical. Moral. Completely unlike his father. He'd been angry at the world and sick of entitled celebrities. Entitled and wealthy men just like his father. Then she'd come along, and he'd met someone who still had a heart despite fame, money, and all that she'd been through.

He patted the jewelry box with the ruby-studded charm necklace he'd purchased in Carmel. Oh, she would remember him, one way or another. Tonight, he would make sure of it. She thought he was nothing but a cowboy, and that was mostly true. But she didn't realize that with the purchase of this working cattle ranch, before long he'd be a billionaire. Billionaire rancher. Yup. He liked the sound of that. Suited him. Nothing wrong with a little ambition. His years of hard work had finally paid off.

Every time she wore this necklace, she'd remember him. Hell, maybe that was selfish, but he didn't care. He couldn't have her, so he'd leave something of himself with her. As the years went by, he figured he'd see her perform on TV and listen to her on the radio. Watch her win the multiple awards she deserved. Someday, she'd get married, probably to another musician, as that seemed to work best in the industry. She'd have children with that guy. Whatever. He couldn't think about any of that right now. Long as she was happy. That's all that mattered.

He knocked on the door to her cottage, and she opened

it, looking nothing like the hung-over kid he'd met not too long ago.

"You always clean up so well." Her gaze slid over the dark suit he wore, this time paired with his favorite black cowboy boots and yes, his black Stetson. "Cowboy."

She looked good enough to eat, and he didn't miss the fact that she wore the infamous titty dress. He swallowed hard, remembering she'd said she would wear that dress for her man.

You're not her man. Remember that.

"Yeah, I know." She looked down at the dress and smirked. "But I'm wearing a jacket that covers my girls well."

That was a relief because even though he had a table reserved at the most romantic restaurant in town, he didn't exactly want her on display to the waiters. They wouldn't be able to concentrate any more than he would be able to tonight.

"Good. Let's get going."

He helped her on with the black sweater and then drove them downtown, past the wharf and Cannery Row. The night was lit up with the fairy lights strung throughout downtown and the pier.

"You didn't *have* to take me out to dinner, you know," she said.

"I have to eat, and I'm tired of pizza, clam chowder, and what's left of the afternoon hors d' oeuvres. I need real food. Like a steak."

"You think only steak is real food?" She laughed. "You're funny, cowboy."

He felt a grin coming on and fought it like a prize fighter. "Rancher, babe. Rancher."

"Either way."

He managed to score front-row parking at the Whaling

Station Steakhouse, took her hand, and tugged her along. "C'mon. You're slowing me down."

"It's these strappy shoes. I can't walk too well in them."

"Should have worn those red boots."

"Yeah, well, I do know how much you like them, but they don't go with everything."

When she stopped for the third time to adjust the strap, he'd had enough. He swept her up in his arms and carried her the rest of the way. Yeah, they got a few looks. He didn't care.

"Hey, is that—" he heard someone say and walked faster.

The last thing he wanted was for her to be recognized with him. He intended to swiftly move out of her life, leaving zero damage in his wake.

"What a ride," she said when he deposited her in front of the hostess stand.

The hostess grinned at them, her gaze lighting only briefly on Sabrina before it landed on him. She made no secret of her interest, licking her lips and brazenly eyeing him.

"I know, he's handsome, isn't he?" Sabrina piped up beside him.

"Huh? Oh, sure, Miss Wilder," the busted hostess answered.

"But he's a cowboy," Sabrina said, sticking out her bottom lip. "Oh, well. Nobody's perfect."

He grinned. "You don't quit this crap you're shoveling, and I'll take you over my knee like I promised."

"Ha! Try it and you'll be walking like you've been on the rodeo circuit for a year."

"Is that a promise? Trouble walking could be taken both ways. If that's an offer, I'm in."

The hostess raised her brows at their banter and walked

them to their table without another word. The table, as he'd requested, was tucked in the back of the restaurant for privacy and intimacy.

He pulled out Sabrina's chair and the hostess left them with their menus. "I'll get your waiter."

"Thanks, Rebecca," Sabrina said as she left, then leaned in close, and stage whispered. "I went to school with her, and she hated me. Now I'm *Miss Wilder*."

"She hated you?"

She shrugged. "It wasn't like she was the only one. It's tough making friends when you're on the road so much."

He pictured a tiny blonde spitfire without any friends. The tightness in his chest wasn't welcome. "Everything is different now. And it will get better every day. You're going to have more good friends than you'll know what to do with."

"Sure," she said, doing a good job of fooling him into believing her. But the doubt was in her eyes, soft and vulnerable.

He knew how it went. From this point forward, it would be even tougher to make solid and real friendships. People would want to get close simply to get status. But she'd have her family around to protect her. He didn't have to be concerned. He refused to worry.

This was as good a time as any to give her a gift that would make her smile. "Remember that western belt buckle you got me?"

"Heck, yeah. I haven't seen you wearing it yet." She smirked, perusing the menu.

"I didn't get you anything in Hollywood." He pulled out the jewelry box and placed it on the table between them. "Now I did."

Her eyes widened, and that's when he realized how much the freaking box looked like a ring box. *Idiot, idiot,*

idiot. "It's a necklace," he explained quickly, breaking out in a cold sweat.

"Oh," she said, taking the box. "That's so nice. You didn't have to."

"I have something to remember you by. Told you I'd always keep the buckle. I hope you'll always keep this." He held his breath while she opened the box and pulled out the ruby-studded red western boot charms that were a perfect likeness of the ones she owned.

She held it strung between her fingers, lightly touching the boots, and smiling from ear to ear.

"You like it, Sunshine?"

"It's perfect."

"You'll wear it?"

"Of course I will. Even if *you* don't wear the buckle."

"Mine is nicer." He stood to help clasp it on her neck, just barely resisting the urge to follow it with a kiss.

"Thank you, Damien. This is considerate and sensitive. So unlike you."

"I'm going to pretend that wasn't an arrow straight into my right ventricle."

"Seriously?" She went narrowed eyes on him.

"I can be *sensitive*."

"You can be, yes. And you also told me that's not who you are." She quirked a brow.

"Fair enough," he said, distracting himself with the menu. He would have a big fat steak tonight. The energy would be needed for what he'd planned for her later.

When the waiter came he ordered the T-bone, rare, and a bottle of Chardonnay because that's what she preferred. She followed suit and ordered a steak. Porterhouse, well done. He tried not to judge her. She wasn't a big red meat fan from what he could tell. And as she'd eloquently stated, nobody was perfect.

"Isn't it going to be hard owning all those cows and then eating steak?"

"I don't name them. They're not pets."

"It's just...sad."

"Yet no one cries when they pick up a steak at the grocery store. Look, I'll make sure my cattle are well taken care of, but when you're a rancher, they're commodities."

"Bessie?" she teased. "A commodity?"

"There's a lot of money in cattle. I'm going to be a billionaire."

"Cool."

If she was impressed, she didn't show it. Then again, Sabrina Wilder had met her share of billionaires, he was certain. She wouldn't impress easily. He appreciated the fact that she didn't think any differently of him, at the same time as he silently wished she'd be impressed. What the hell was wrong with him?

After they were served, they ate mostly in silence. Sabrina appeared a little more reserved than normal, occasionally fingering the ruby red boots. He wondered what she was thinking but thought better than to ask. She couldn't have expected a ring from him, nor would she have wanted one. He couldn't picture her happy on a ranch in Texas with him. Neither one of them should compromise their future for what would amount to a risk that wouldn't pay off long term. If that sounded like a businessman, it was the way he'd lived his life. He couldn't change now midstream. She was a high risk. *They* were a high risk.

He pictured them living together for any length of time and figured they'd kill each other before long. Though it might be a nice way to go.

"Are you ready?" he asked after he'd paid and given the waiter a generous tip for staying out of their way as much as possible.

He drove them back to the B&B as Sabrina sat beside him and continued to touch the charm like it was a worry stone or a talisman. Her thoughts were nearly loud enough for him to hear.

He parked the sedan and turned to her. "I can hear you thinking."

"What am I thinking?" She turned to him, eyes shimmering in the soft moonlight.

"That you can't wait to get inside and knock boots." He grinned.

"That sounds like what you're thinking."

"You got me." He curled his fingers around the nape of her neck, lightly touching the necklace.

"I was realizing, actually, that this is the first real date I've ever been on. And it was really nice."

The words hit him hard. She had to be kidding. "What do you mean the first date?"

"Well, the first grown-up date. I mean, I had a few dates when I was a teenager. The bowling alley. Fast food. And there were a couple of business dates. New and up-and-coming Nashville stars the label wanted to be seen with me, so we went to the CMAs together. Stuff like that. Not that they weren't all very nice, but they didn't like me. A couple of them even had girlfriends back home."

"I'm...speechless. I guess you're not counting Hollywood."

"No, because you *had* to take me there. It was business, and you were my escort. Tonight you didn't have to do any of this. Not even to get lucky."

"You're right. Didn't have to do any of it. Just wanted to."

She turned to him, positioning her knees so they pointed to him. "Was I a good date as these things go?"

He tipped her chin. "You did everything a man wants his date to do. Embarrass the hostess who was hitting on him and threaten his balls if he should dare to hurt you. You not only ordered a steak but ate it, even though it was damn near charred. Gotta say, I'm pretty proud."

Not to mention humbled. He'd given her something to remember him by, but it turned out he was the one who'd remember her, and by much more than the gift. It scared him spitless, too, because with each passing minute she burrowed further and further under his skin.

And leaving wasn't going to be easy anymore.

20

"Independence Day" by Martina McBride

Sabrina had never worn anything as beautiful as the gold necklace with the red boots charm. Oh, she'd worn plenty of expensive jewelry on loan. Cartier and others had loved her to wear their gorgeous bling on the red carpet, when presenting awards, or on promotional photo shoots. But none of that had ever been hers. Her parents didn't believe in their daughters owning expensive jewelry before their wedding day. They'd doted on Sabrina and her sisters in many other ways.

But this piece of jewelry was *hers,* and it was gorgeous. She knew it was expensive, but she didn't care about that. The only thing that mattered was that he'd wanted her to have it. It was sentimental in nature. She couldn't stop touching it, reliving the moment. For one second, forever suspended in time, she'd seen that box and thought it could be a ring. In the space of what might have been half a second, she'd gone through a range of emotions. Happy, worried, terrified. She'd pictured life on a ranch and life on the road. A big wedding and children. And then she'd witnessed the horrified look on his face, which slapped her out of the crazy, stupid fantasy.

They barely knew each other.

Even if it wasn't a ring, this was beautiful, and it *meant* something. She didn't know what it meant to him, which was part of what she'd been trying to figure out on the drive home. He didn't love her. She understood. If he did, he would have said something by now. It's not like he kept stuff from her, whether she wanted to hear about it or not. At least she'd been a "good" date. Although she wasn't sure if anyone other than him would appreciate what she'd done. But she couldn't take Rebecca eye-fucking Damien right in front of her, like Sabrina didn't even exist! Good to know he hadn't cared for it either.

Now, Damien was seated on her fluffy couch in the adjoining living room. In the same spot he'd been when she'd tried on her new wardrobe for him as he sat, legs spread out, acting like the judge of the entire world. And now, here she stood, wearing the banned dress. For *him*. She may as well, since it could be years before she had someone else to wear it for. And somehow it seemed right for it to be him.

He'd already given her so much.

"C'mere." He beckoned to her.

She kicked off her strappy heels and climbed on his lap. This hiked the dress up a little higher than decent which was just fine with her.

"Hi," she said, pulling off his hat and tossing it to the side. She threaded her fingers through his thick, dark hair.

"Dayum, baby, this dress. Why didn't I want you to have it?" His fingers slowly traced along the edge, to the flesh of her cleavage, lingering a while before lowering to cup her breast.

"The boobage." That small touch set her on fire and she sighed. "Too indecent."

"But again, *why* didn't I think you should have it?"

She tossed her hair back, giving him better access. "Image, cowboy. Image."

"Yeah...that's...important." His breaths became ragged, and he busied himself kissing her neck, tugging on her earlobe, and pulling her closer.

She was already half undressed and, wanting him to join her yesterday, she unbuttoned his shirt and quickly stripped it off. She skimmed his beautiful taut pecs down to his abs, enjoying when his muscles tightened and tensed under her touch. Her hands rested on the waistband of his black jeans, and she tugged.

"Patience." His large hand settled on hers, and in one quick movement, he flipped them. She wound up under him. "Let me."

He kissed her, long and deep, wet and warm. No one kissed like he did. No one. Her body tingled, on fire for him within seconds. In no time at all, her dress was no longer her second skin, and it had been discarded along with her underwear. Instead he was on her skin, all over with his tongue, his lips, touring and exploring her.

Pulled under again like he was her undertow, she slowly lost herself to him. But she had to say something to him first. She had to tell him. The thought had ruminated in her mind the entire ride home. It was a risk, but one she would take. If there was anything her life had taught her well, it was that some risks were well worth taking. And at this point, she had little left to lose since she'd already lost her heart.

He was doing something diabolical to her belly button with his tongue, and it took a Herculean effort to consider distracting him now.

"Damien."

"What, baby?" But he didn't stop what he was doing.

"Damien."

"You don't like this?" He stopped, but continued south, his tongue leading the way.

"Damien!" she shouted before she changed her mind.

She had his attention now as he stopped everything and braced himself above her, meeting her eyes. "You okay?"

"Yes." She framed his face with her hands, those breathtaking, dark eyes warm and now questioning. "I know you don't fall in love. But you should know *this* is special to me. I didn't think it would be, not quite like this. I—"

"Sun—"

Finger to his lips, she shushed him. His eyes widened, but he remained quiet.

"Wait. Let me say this. You made me feel like myself again. I almost forgot that girl, and who she was, but you brought her right out of me. I found myself all over again. Just me. All the sass and spit, because you pissed me off so much."

He tried to talk, but she covered his mouth with her entire hand this time, and it was a muffled sound. It sounded a little like, "...talented...that way."

"Because you asked if singing was what I wanted to do with my life, for the first time I know it's what I want. I chose this time, it didn't choose me."

Again, he mumbled under her hand.

"Shhh."

He rolled his eyes.

"I won't ever forget you. No matter how far away we are

from each other. And I'll always compare everyone else to you." She removed her hand from his lips.

"Baby." His eyes were soft, and his voice was a deep and grating sound that touched her heart. "I'm going to make you feel so good tonight you'll have that benchmark set very high."

"Oh, yeah?"

"You better make sure never to lower it...ever. Because this is nothing less than you deserve. Every. Fucking. Night."

Oh. My. God.

Just the thought of having him to herself every night, like this, and she was nearly a melted pool of bones on the floor. Slowly, and as if he meant to stretch the moment out into next year, he kissed her. His hot tongue met hers, urging, demanding. She met his urgency, desperate for more of him. Her fingers clawed at his firm, steely shoulders, pulling him closer still.

When they came up for air, she smiled and said, "Take your pants off and stay for a while."

He did, quickly rising to divest himself of his pants and underwear. She licked her lips at the sight of all that now naked, sinewy, and hard manly beauty. Wide capable shoulders and a chiseled chest tapered to his waist and stunning V muscles. Then, possibly her favorite part, large, bulging, and ready for her. That breath stealing man was on her again, and they were skin on skin. Belly to belly. Moving and sliding against each other in a wild tangle of limbs. He lowered his head and his mouth was on her breast, teasing and suckling her nipple until it was one hard peak. Not ignoring the other breast, he gave each one equal attention, suckling tenderly and then not so tenderly, causing her to writhe under him.

She reached between them for him, stroking him until he groaned. "I'm not going to make you wait tonight."

He covered himself with a condom and entered her in one deep thrust that made them both gasp. His slow movements inside of her were strokes that had a fire building deep in her belly. The fire spread and traveled down her legs and in-between her thighs. Her breath caught and then caught again when she gripped his buttocks and urged him to go faster. Deeper. He responded to her need, and the fire stoked. The pressure and friction inside of her rose, and an electrical current pulsated and spread through her body and all the way to her toes. She couldn't hold back any longer as the hot sting of orgasm claimed her, and she bucked beneath him.

Her long orgasm seemed to milk his own, and he followed her over, his hold on her tightening as he drove into her.

MUCH LATER, she laid in his arms, sated, warm and...safe.

They'd raided her freezer for ice cream and eaten it in bed. Damien's experiment with ice cream on her skin made her more than a little sticky but in a happy way. They took a shower together after that and didn't leave before having wild monkey sex. She didn't want this night to end. Maybe, just this once, they could have the whole night. To spoon. Cuddle. He had his stupid rule that she hated. But tonight was different. Special. He might feel it, too. It might be selfish and asking too much, but she didn't believe so.

And she was going to ask, God help her.

She pressed a kiss to his warm neck. "Will you please spend the night with me?"

He nuzzled her temple and took only a moment to reply. "Yeah."

Then he rolled to his side and tucked her back to his front. "Now go to sleep." He lightly slapped her bottom.

"I love you," Sabrina said into the darkness of the room. He didn't respond but he did tug her even tighter to him.

And Sabrina, who always had a difficult time falling asleep before two a.m., was asleep within minutes.

She woke the next morning to the aroma of freshly brewed coffee. Opening one eye and pushing a lock of hair out of her face, she caught a picturesque sight. Damien, his shirt on but still unbuttoned, revealing tanned and sinewy flesh. He wore his slacks, too, but his hair was damp like he'd just showered.

She propped up on one elbow. "Aren't you jogging this morning?"

"No time," he said and handed her a coffee mug, placing a quick kiss on her shoulder.

She sipped the warm, dark liquid, trying to jostle her brain. If he'd mentioned his plans last night, she was clearly blanking out. "What's going on?"

"Turns out my travel agent got me an earlier flight to Dallas. I'm leaving today on standby. Got to get to the airport."

Casually, like he just hadn't ripped her heart out, he buttoned his shirt.

She shot up straight, no longer requiring mere caffeine to wake her the hell up. "Today? But what about...we had... we have two more nights at least."

"Got to get to Dallas and sign my contract. You'll be signing yours soon enough."

"That's it? I've got my contract coming, so you're leaving?"

"That *was* the plan."

She sucked in a breath, the pain taking all of the oxygen from her lungs. *It had been the plan before.* Before he'd given her the charm. Before she'd said she loved him. Before he'd spent the night with her. And maybe that was the whole problem.

She rolled out of bed, found her bathrobe and shoved it on, tying the belt on with jerky movements. "I see what you're doing. You spent the night, and that was too much for you. Now you have to go because you don't *do* love, and this looks too much like love to you."

He wouldn't look at her. "You knew this was happening. I was straight with you."

He had been. But everything had changed, and he *had* to feel it. Suddenly it became all too clear to her. She'd done it again. Allowed herself to feel too much. To hope too much. Hope that her friends hadn't forgotten all about her when she came back from a month on the road. Hope her boyfriend wouldn't cheat because she'd been gone for months. Yeah. Pointless hope.

Just because she felt this incredible intensity for him didn't mean he felt the same.

"Sure," she said, feeling defeated again. "You were honest. Thanks for that."

Stupid, silly, and naïve Sabrina all over again. This time not because someone had tricked and humiliated her, but because she'd done this to herself.

"Baby," he said, tugging on the belt of her bathrobe. "I think you know I'm going to miss you like hell. But this was the deal. From the start. Nothing's changed."

Nothing's changed.

"That's okay," she said, swiping at the tears that had

trickled out. "You'll come and visit me in Nashville. Or I'll come out to see your ranch."

He pressed his forehead to hers. "No. This is a clean break. You're going to be busy with your new life. It's a fresh start for you, and you don't need an old cowboy like me dragging you down."

She pressed palms against his chest, pushing him. "Don't you tell me what I need. I don't want to do this without you."

"You will." He tipped her chin to meet his eyes. "I'm going to watch you do it from a distance and be right proud of you."

"No, Damien. Don't do this. Please."

"This is the deal. I have to let you go." And then he did let her go, grabbed his jacket and his keys and headed for the door. "Bye, Sunshine."

She didn't say her goodbye until he shut the door. Then, because some part of her still didn't believe he wouldn't come running back in here and tell her it had all been a terrible mistake, she watched through her front window. A few minutes later, he walked to the parking lot, carrying his suitcase, threw it in the trunk, and drove off. Out of her life. That easy.

The arrogant man she'd hated. If only she could have stayed hating him, then this all might be much easier to take. But she'd be okay. Sure, she would. She'd faced worse in her life. Or more to the point, she'd had her heart ripped out once or twice before. This time it stung with a pain she felt physically. It pressed on her heart, making it difficult to breathe.

Sabrina picked up her cell phone and dialed. "Hey, Jessie?" She sniffed into the phone. "You busy?"

"Of course, I am. But I'm right outside your door. Just open it."

Dropping her phone, Sabrina flew to the door, tore it open, and went into her big sister's arms. "Oh, Jessie. You were right."

Then, because loud sobs were shaking her body, Jessie didn't say anything. She just held on to Sabrina, patting her back and stroking her hair like their mother used to do when they'd had the flu. When the sobs became hiccups, Jessie sat Sabrina on the couch and went into the kitchen. She came back with a mug of what appeared to be hot chocolate, as it had whipped cream on top.

"Here," she said and handed it to Sabrina.

She took a sip, noting it was coffee, and making a face at the unexpected combination of coffee and whipped cream.

Jessie shrugged. "You didn't have hot chocolate."

Hot chocolate had been another comfort during bad times. "It's actually delicious."

Sabrina sipped quietly while Jessie waited for her to be able to talk. "How...how did you know?"

"I checked him out when he left. Kind of knew I would find you in this state."

"I'm sorry," Sabrina felt the need to apologize. "It's just... the timing."

"A few days early?"

"No," Sabrina said, sniffing and swiping a tear away. "After I told him I loved him. That's when he chooses to leave."

Jessie straightened, lips thin and tight. "What? Right after you told him?"

"Well, no. Not right after. But close enough."

"And what did he say?"

"Nothing." She should have known then, but something

unnamed kept pressing at her brain. He wasn't telling her the whole truth.

"Oh, honey."

"I know, Jessie. I'm a dummy. But I figured I had nothing left to lose but my pride." And bam, there went that, too! Heart, goodbye. Hello pride, see ya later.

"It is strange," Jessie mused. "Because I was beginning to think he really cared about you. A couple of days ago, I had been talking with Lexi, and she handed the phone to Luke. He wanted me to let D.C. know to go ahead and send him a bill for the wardrobe, the trip to Hollywood, everything else. When I asked D.C., he said to tell Luke it's taken care of. So, all this time he spent here is on his own dime. That's hardly a way to retire."

"He has money," Sabrina said.

But she'd also noticed he'd gone far beyond what she'd thought an image consultant would. She simply figured that's just how he worked. Now she wondered. Then she remembered something he'd told her in his own words. *Listen to what people are not saying as much as what they are.* And Damien hadn't said he loved her, but he'd certainly shown her. In many different ways.

One of them being walking away so she could move forward in her new life.

Sabrina rubbed her charms, and Jessie noticed them for the first time. "Pretty."

"He gave this to me last night."

Jessie moved closer and inspected the charm. "Seriously? This is expensive, Sabrina. Are these...are these real rubies?"

"I think so." She knew it. She'd worn rubies before. Real rubies were different from rhinestones because imitations could never be the real thing.

"Wow. I don't get it. This man does so much for your career, presumably does care about you, gives you this beautiful and expensive jewelry—"

"Don't forget sentimental. They're supposed to be my red boots, which he loves."

Jessie just gawked at her. "And then he just walks right out of your life? Who does that?"

"I don't know. A stubborn, arrogant man?"

"Sabrina, I think he loves you."

"It doesn't matter. He doesn't *want* to love me. He's gone."

"That's because men, who are supposed to be stronger, are weak as hell." She pointed to her chest. "We're the weaker sex, or so people say, but that's a load of crap. We're the ones with hearts like a lion. They're the ones who run with fear."

Sabrina knew that her sister was right. This big man was too afraid to love her.

The hot spike of anger rose up in her then and spread through her heart, taking over the place of her pain.

21
———

"Don't Take the Girl" by Tim McGraw

*J*ust keep driving. Don't look back. Don't you do it, idiot.

That's exactly what D.C. did as he took Highway 156 north headed toward Highway 101 and the San Jose International Airport. Unable to sleep since five a.m., for a while he'd simply watched Sabrina doze. She looked like a freaking *Playboy* centerfold sprawled out on the bed. Naked. Blonde hair spread out like a halo. Sleeping like she lived. Like she kissed. Like she loved. Like she sang. All in.

Raw emotions rolled through him, constricted his chest, and made it hard to be logical. But logic was all he had to cling to right now. This wouldn't work. It couldn't work. He'd employed logic at the crack of dawn, called his travel agent, and she'd gotten him on a stand-by flight. He'd spend all day in the airport if he had to, but he had to get back to

Texas. He had to be the one to walk away because she was too kind and loving to do it for herself.

This was why he should have never gotten involved. It was too much. Too much frail emotion he despised. Weakness like he'd seen in his mother. Fear like he hadn't experienced since the day he'd approached the sperm donor, hoping to be rescued. The anger and hostility had been easier. Comfortable. Had the added benefit of usually keeping people at a distance.

Most people, it turned out. Not all.

He could now add damned coward to his resume. Running was better than facing the mess he'd left behind. He hadn't screwed up like this in a long while, if ever. And out of all the self-entitled celebrities he could have harmed, it had been *Sabrina*. Someone he hadn't wanted to hurt. Tried his best not to harm. He was supposed to have slid into and out of her life easily.

Somewhere it had all slipped out of control. Thing is, he knew when it had started to veer, and he'd been unable to stop. He'd allowed her to tempt him, to get under his skin until he couldn't resist her. Fail number one. Next, he'd let sentiment and his own powerful emotions get the better of him and bought the expensive charm. Fail number two. Lastly, he'd spent the night, knowing what it meant to her. Fail number three. Before he got to fail number number four and be forced to kick his own ass, he dropped off the sedan at the car rental and headed through TSA and to the terminal to wait.

One hour turned into two, which turned into three. He paced the floor. Checked his emails, refreshing like a maniac, then finally settled to going through his photos, deleting old ones of ranches he wouldn't be buying. He'd forgotten the most recent photos he'd taken were of the

Hollywood tour with Sabrina. And there they were in front of him. Photos of her beautiful smiling face hamming it up on the Walk of Fame, fisting the rock on sign, sticking her tongue out at him. Then the selfies he'd taken of them in front of the Hollywood billboard in the hills.

He caught the look she gave him when his face was turned to face the camera but hers was turned to him. Adoring. She'd loved him even then. Crazy. These two people looked like a couple. They looked like they'd been together for years and not days.

Maybe sometimes it happened that way. Maybe two people who barely knew each other could connect on a deeper level than he'd believed possible.

No. No, that didn't make any sense.

What was happening to him?

"This is crazy," he said, dragging a hand through his hair as he put his phone away.

"Not really," said a kid lying on the floor next to him using his backpack as a pillow. "I once waited all night on standby. Dude, this is nothing."

Yeah, not what he meant. He shouldn't be sitting here occupying space when he could be with Sabrina. When he could finally man up and tell her how he felt. Let her make the decision as to where they could go from there. Take a risk with his heart for once.

"I'm an idiot," he said, standing.

"Wow. That's kind of harsh."

Harsh or not, it was the truth. He ordered a car, then waited outside. Checking his wristwatch incessantly, he finally left the airport for the hour plus drive back to Monterey Bay.

"Are you new to California?" the driver asked kindly.

"No, I was just here a few hours ago."

"Great! Miss us?"

"Actually, I never left."

"Oh, yeah? What's up with that?"

"Nothing. I'm just losing my mind."

More like his heart.

Why not, since Sabrina had obviously lost her heart to him first. And she'd have to have lost her mind to love him. A harsh cowboy who'd never given her any reason to trust him with her heart. But she had because that's who she was. She still didn't know how to put up a wall that would stay up. She needed his help and protection from those who would use her. Face it, whether she needed it or not, she was getting it. Getting him, if she'd still have him. But unless she was one fickle woman, a few hours shouldn't have changed her mind. She loved him, and she'd had the guts to tell him so when he hadn't.

Love didn't always make a person weak. Sometimes it made someone strong enough to take a risk.

He finally arrived in Whistle Cove, grabbed his luggage, and headed to her cottage. Banging on the door, he called her name. He was about to break the door down when he got a hold of himself. She was probably not inside anyway.

He walked to the check-in desk, finding Jessie there.

"I'm back. Where's Sabrina?"

"I'm not going to tell you." She pursed her lips together. "You made her cry. Now go away. I have no rooms left."

"Let's not do this. You know I'll get to her if I have to tear her door down. If I have to tear down every door in this place."

"Don't you dare! Doors are expensive."

"Then tell me where she is right now."

Jessie came around from behind the check in area, hand

on hips. "Listen, *sir*. I'm very *nice* until you hurt my sister. The nice wears off after that."

"Got it. But how am I supposed to fix this if you don't tell me where she is right now?"

"I have no idea, but it's not my problem, now, is it?"

"Fine, I'll start knocking doors down." He picked up his bag.

"Wait. You don't have to do that. You didn't hear this from me, but she might be cleaning the Sea Captain room. We already have your vacancy filled."

"That was fast." Leaving his bag, he bounded up the steps to his room and stopped cold at the entrance.

Sabrina was there with her mother, bending over the bed, tucking in the last corner of the sheet. She stood back and admired her work. "I did it! I did it!"

She bounced in place, clapped her hands, and hugged her mother.

"Sabrina," he said from the doorway, heart in his throat.

Both women turned to him, but Sabrina stared like she'd seen a ghost. Her eyes widened, then softened, then filled with tears, then narrowed. The four stages of Sabrina Wilder. For the love of his ranch, he loved this woman.

And it no longer scared the spit out of him to admit it.

"What are you doing here? Did you miss your flight?" Sabrina asked.

"If you'll excuse me, please," Kit Wilder said, brushing past him.

"Don't you dare go anywhere, Mom," Sabrina said, fists on her hips.

Yeah, she wasn't going to make it easy. Good for her. That was *his* woman, right there.

"But, I have to—" Kit began.

"No!" Sabrina said.

"Yes," D.C. ordered and turned to Kit. "Please."

"Honey," Kit said to Sabrina. "It's just that Olga needs me in the kitchen. I'm sorry."

Sabrina called after her mother, "Olga *never* needs you. That is a bald-faced lie!"

D.C. shut the door to his former room. Sabrina gave him her back and paired it with a loud "Humph!"

"Let me talk to you, baby."

"No! You left. I told you I loved you, and you left."

"Made a mistake. What, you never made a mistake?" Yeah, he figured that would get her attention. Like him, she'd made a few.

They were two of a kind in some ways.

She turned again to face him, and he took in the fact that she hadn't removed the necklace. He let it settle inside, calming his last nerve. He was going to take that as a good sign, even if it had just been a few hours. She had likely taken a shower, dressed, and still she wore it. Yeah, she was going to forgive him.

Eventually.

"You're still wearing the necklace," he said softly.

Her fingers played with the charm and she shrugged. "Yeah, well, it's bling."

"I know how you like your bling." For now, he would go ahead and pretend he believed that it was nothing more than a piece of jewelry to her. They both knew better.

"You shouldn't have left me this morning. It was horrible timing. Right after I told you I loved you. Right after we spent the night together. You're...you're mean!"

"Not mean," he corrected. "I'm a bastard. But a lucky one. I don't know why you love me, but you do."

"I have my reasons." She sniffed and tipped her chin as if to defend her position.

Had he mentioned how much he loved this woman?

He stepped into her, crowding her, not willing to let her go. "Sunshine, give me another chance."

"Why should I?"

"Because you love me," he said, and tugged her by the nape of her neck close enough to share a breath.

"So?" He waited until she met his gaze. Her eyes were the warmest green. They were no longer flashing him bolts of anger but were back to mild irritation.

Right where they began. He could work with that. "And because I love you."

"Really?" A hopeful smile tugged at her lips, and right then he wanted to give her everything he had. "You mean you're going to actually admit it?"

"Wait. What?" This was supposed to be news to her. It was news to him. He'd never loved anyone like this before.

If that made him weak, well, he was going to learn to live with it.

"Damien, you need to take your own advice. I know you love me. You told me to listen to what people *don't* tell you as much as what they do tell you. You didn't tell me, but you showed me. You took care of me, and you protected me. You stayed here longer than you had to, and you helped me more than you had to. I also know that you wouldn't even take Luke's money. Everything you did was for me. I wasn't just a job to you anymore. And then there's this necklace." She touched it tenderly. "I know you love me."

"I do love you. I wish you'd told me sooner and not left me in the dark."

She laughed. "You had to figure this out for yourself. Plus, you wouldn't have believed me."

"Okay. Maybe you're right."

"You don't 'do love,' remember?"

"No. I don't fall in love. Just this once." He pulled her to him, breathing in her sweet scent.

She climbed him. "I knew it! Congratulations, baby. You're not one of the weak ones!"

"Thanks?" He nuzzled her neck. "You've already figured out so much, have you figured out what we're going to do? You don't like ranches or cows. Said so yourself."

"But I do love horses." She batted her eyelashes. "And I especially love cowboys."

"Baby, I think I can help you with that."

EPILOGUE

"I Love You" by Martina McBride

Austin, Texas, two months later

S abrina finished the night's set performing her new release, "No Excuses, This is Me," a somewhat toned-down version of the song Lexi had written for Sabrina's debut album. No longer a song about an angry, vengeful woman taking a bat to her ex's car—and, metaphorically, the press— this one was about a woman grabbing her second chance. Tonight she and her back-up band had played to a sell-out crowd at Austin Beat.

It was a small venue, but she was proud of the fact that she'd packed it headlining the show. The label had scheduled her for a few shows in strategic areas to test the market, and so far, the response had been better than they could have hoped. Sabrina still had fans, loyal ones who'd stayed with her through the toughest and most painful time of her career. Yet in all that hurt had come amazing growth.

This was, by far, the sweetest time of her life.

Best of all, tonight was their last show for a while, so she'd go home to Damien's ranch, and they'd have some private time for a few weeks before she had to head into a Nashville recording studio. She'd been a frequent visitor to the D.C. Ranch, spending long, luxurious weekends with him. Her first surprise had been that the ranch was less like a farm with a red barn and more like a sprawling compound with a house big enough to get lost in.

When Damien had first driven her to the place so far on the outskirts of Dallas that she thought they were already in another state, she'd thought he'd decided they would spend the night at a resort. But no, he'd driven her past the looming D.C. Ranch sign into his cattle ranch, apparently the second largest in Texas. Damien was super serious about this cowboy business, she'd come to learn.

"Good show," Sabrina said, fist bumping with the guitar player backstage and handing her mike to Jerry, one of their roadies.

"See you in a few weeks, Sabrina," said their drummer, Adam. "Rest up and say hi to D.C. for us."

They'd all met him, of course. Damien was a little on the protective side and didn't want her hanging with a bunch of hot guys until they'd met him, too. She understood. Lucky for her, none of Damien's many young ranch hands were women. So far, though, Damien swore he wouldn't discriminate if a woman really wanted the job. He'd promised to allow her to do the interviewing, she was sure just to humor her.

She had no idea who would be a good ranch hand and who would be a lousy one. She was still learning her way around a cattle ranch, but she already had her own quarter horse. The second surprise. A gift from Damien, she'd named him Boots. He was a sweet boy. She hadn't ridden Boots yet as she first had to learn how to groom and saddle him.

It also turned out that Damien had a lot more money than she'd ever imagined. She'd first learned of just how much more when he'd bought her a truck just to better get around the property. The third surprise. It wasn't a small pick-up truck as she'd expected, but a fully loaded 4x4. In red, of course. Private joke.

Damien met her at the stage door, and she was so happy to see him, she did a running jump into his arms. "Baby. Oh, wow, I missed you."

"Not more than I missed you."

"Did you catch the show?"

He nodded. "You were amazing as always."

"You're just biased." She removed his Stetson and ruffled his hair.

And he carried her just that way with her legs wrapped around his waist, as if she was light as cotton candy, outside to the parking lot and his waiting 4x4. They passed a small crowd of onlookers held back by a privacy rope. He opened the passenger door, buckled her in, then kissed her long and deep.

"I've been waiting for that," she whispered against his lips.

"Been waiting for a lot more." His dark eyes heated and shimmered.

She smirked. "I know. Me, too. We have three weeks, and we're not getting out of bed for the first two days."

Within minutes, they were pulling out onto the highway and the more than three-hour drive to the ranch. Sabrina set the station to one of the country channels and leaned her head on his shoulder, her hand on his thigh. She would snooze most of the drive.

"We're stopping for a late dinner," Damien announced within minutes.

She leaned back, surprised. "But what will Lucille say?"

Lucille was Damien's hired cook, a sixty-year-old woman, and she was like Olga on steroids. She insisted they eat at home every night because only she could feed them "good ol' Texas home cookin'."

"She'll be fine. I've been wanting to get you out on a date again." His big palm settled on her knee.

It had been a while, and though Sabrina was tired and ready for bed, she didn't want to complain or make excuses. She'd waited so long to see him again, this man who she loved so desperately at times she didn't know what to do when they were apart.

"Okay. Let's go to dinner."

Not surprisingly, a few minutes later he pulled the truck into a local steakhouse.

As usual, he helped her down from her seat, so she wouldn't have to jump down. He blocked her in, bracing his arms on either side of her. He was sex on a stick with his rumpled dark hair and bristled jawline, and she wasn't too tired to want to ravage him right in the parking lot.

"Are you going to do it tonight?" he asked.

She knew exactly what "it" he referred to. "Ugh. Really?"

"You promised."

It was true. She'd promised him she'd expand her beef-eating horizons. "Fine. I don't know why it's so important to you. I'll have the steak medium-rare."

"Thanks, baby. It kills me to see the way you eat steak."

Her mind distracted by the pink meat she'd have to eat,

she tried not to allow her churning stomach to get the better of her. She'd wash it down with some Coke or Pepsi and prove to him that she'd tried, but she didn't like it. Her meat had to be cooked enough not to be able to walk off the table by itself, thank you very much.

Damien tugged on her hand, leading her to the back of the restaurant and then into a private room. There were already rows of tables with people seated, and it took her all of three minutes to recognize them. Lexi and Luke were seated next to Jessie and Mom. Even Gran was there with her gentleman friend, Sir Clint.

"Hey!" she squealed. "What are y'all doing here?"

Yes, she was talking like a Texan now.

"Surprise," Damien said, from behind her.

"Who's running the B&B?" It was the first question she'd thought to ask. Obviously, they'd all come out to congratulate her on the success of the first few shows.

"We left Olga and Tony in charge," Jessie said.

"We just had to be here." Lexi grinned.

"I'm so happy for you, honey." Mom waved a hand in front of her face to hold back tears.

Oh boy. A bit of an over-the-top response from her mother. What else was new?

"Thanks, it was a good show tonight. But what a nice surprise!" She turned to Damien to thank him, and he had a tiny velvet box in his hands.

Shock and excitement slammed through her at once, but unlike two months ago, she never shifted to worry. This was no fantasy. In one quick moment she took it all in… there was a tiered cake on a corner table. Everyone she loved in one room. That's when she realized he'd done all this for her. The idea of loving her no longer scared him. They still hadn't known each other for all that long. But this no longer mattered because she'd learned everything that counted.

She'd noticed that for a man who'd once said he didn't "do love," he got cranky if she forgot to tell him that she loved him during a phone call from the road. She'd discovered that he had a heart for all animals, not just horses, and took in abused and injured animals to nurse them back to health. She'd fallen deeper for him on that day and uncovered the most significant lesson of all.

They were made for each other.

"Baby, that better not be another necklace." Her voice shook as she barely held back tears.

He slid her that impossibly striking smile. "Not this time."

He flipped open the box and inside was a breathtaking solitaire diamond surrounded by tiny rubies. Perfect. She sucked in a breath as wet lashes clouded her vision.

"It's so beautiful...it's going to match my boots." She touched the necklace she rarely took off.

Damien "D.C." (to everyone else, that is) Caldwell went down on bended knee. "Sabrina Wilder, will you marry me, please?"

"Yes!" She nearly shouted, pulling him up to his feet. "I think you know I'm yours, and I always will be."

"Counting on it," he said, slipping the ring on her finger. "This seals the deal."

Sabrina held it up in the air, showing it off, before she clung to Damien.

Everyone clapped and cheered. Mom was openly weeping, clutching Gran, who was trying to get away from her. Sir Clint held up both arms in a rally cheer. Lexi and Jessie were hugging. Luke gave Sabrina a sly wink. In a way, her future brother-in-law had been the reason she'd accidentally met the love of her life.

She'd have to thank him later.

For now, she was a little busy. She framed her fiancé's face. "Do you know how I said we're not getting out of bed for two days? Make that five days."

"Holding you to it, baby. Holding you to it."

ALSO BY HEATHERLY BELL:

More from the Wilder Sisters:

Country Gold

A Country Wedding

Country Hot: the anthology

Winning Mr. Charming

Lucky Cowboy

Nashville Cowboy

Built like a Cowboy

More than One Night

Reluctant Hometown Hero

The Right Moment

COMING SOON:

Grand Prize Cowboy

Cowboy, It's Christmas

The Charming Checklist

Please see my website for the full book catalog.

ABOUT THE AUTHOR

Heatherly Bell drinks too much coffee, craves cupcakes, and occasionally wears real pants. She lives in northern California with her family.

You can find her all over social media posting about her dog, and the eternal battle over carbs.